The Amish Garden

Victoria Morton

Published by Trellis Publishing, 2021.

This is a work of fiction. Similarities to real people, places, or events are entirely coincidental.

THE AMISH GARDEN

First edition. July 8, 2021.

Copyright © 2021 Victoria Morton.

ISBN: 979-8224221653

Written by Victoria Morton.

THE AMISH GARDEN

VICTORIA MORTON

1

Benjamin stood in the garden he loved most close to the park and breathed in the scent of the many flowers. He loved the red ones as they reminded him of his parents' love for each other. He listened to his mother scream at the twins as they played in the park and he smiled. Those two were very mischievous but they were his younger brothers and he loved them just as much. It was the evening of his graduation from high school and instead of having a big bash at home in the name of celebration, he'd rather have it out here with nature in the company of the people he loved most his parents and his twin brothers Joseph and Joshua. He peeked from the door that led out of the garden and spotted his aunt Maggie with her husband Gerald. They had just gotten married some months back and had promised to be at his graduation party since she couldn't attend the ceremony due to the much work she had to handle at bakery. Benjamin's dad had a very big bakery business which had been in the family since before his parents were born. The family business had been a small one then while they had been living in their little Amish community in Lancaster County. He had been brought up according to the ways of the *ordnung* alongside his brothers until his parents decided to adopt the *englischer's* way of life. The move wasn't easy as he was just twelve then and had to leave a lot of his friends behind. His dad had moved the family business too and now the bakery was one of the biggest in town. Benjamin had never loved baking but he always talked of handling the business part of the bakery. The business world was enticing and he let it lure him into its possibilities. He was going to start applying for colleges soon and business school was the first on his list of preference. A noise in the far end of the garden brought him out of his fantasies and he went in search of the noise. It stopped when it heard him coming and when he paused to listen to be sure his mind wasn't playing games with his sense of hearing, the noise continued but this time it was low and came in bouts. It sounded like someone sobbing and his human sense kicked in. He began to search frantically for whoever it was asking the person to come out so he could make sure whoever it was, was alright.

"Who's there?" he asked and just immediately the sobs ceased. You can show yourself, I don't bite," he said hoping the person would trust his words or the calmness in his voice and step out into the open. The garden was a large one with twists and turns like a maze. Finding someone who wasn't willing to be found was going to be a lot harder than he thought. He made to take the next turn and nearly ran into a figure standing there with her hair flowing down her back. She had her hand to her face as if in shame.

"Hey there you scared the willies out of me. What are you doing here all by yourself?" She turned to look at him and he backed away his legs alert to take to his heels if it turned out he had run into the famous faerie the caretaker of the garden always said visited the garden to sing to the flowers. He didn't really believe in those things but he had to be on guard anyway.

"I should be asking..." she began to say but suddenly went mute when she saw who it was. She hadn't expected to see him here.

"I'm sorry sir I didn't mean to disturb you. I was actually on my way out." Benjamin was taken aback by her beauty and politeness. Why was she addressing him that way? He was just seventeen an had barely achieved anything life apart from colleges clamoring to have him study in their citadels as one of the best graduating students of his school. He didn't know her from anywhere but she behaved like she had seen him before. He couldn't have missed that look of recognition she had in her eyes before she bowed her head in a bid to look away from him.

"Please tell me you are not the faerie the caretaker speaks about." That statement seemed to amuse her a lot as she threw back her head in laughter. Before long Benjamin was laughing with her. Her laughter was infectious and her smile alone made him want to know everything about her.

"You don't believe in that do you?" she asked this time with her head up and her eyes boring holes into his face.

"No I don't." He replied shrugging his shoulders and making a who'd-ever-believe-that face. The look on your face earlier says you do.

"If you are not the faerie, then who are you?"

"I'm Lovina Lapp."

"Lapp? You are Amish? I'm Amish too." Benjamin said with a hint of excitement in his voice.

"I know. You moved from Lancaster County." Lovina smiled at him. Benjamin was practically dumbfounded. Who was this girl that knew everything about him?

"What don't you know about me?" he asked as he drew closer to her. She drifted back into her silent docile mouse mood and just smiled. Please allow me the pleasure of touring the garden with you as you tell me about yourself. And just immediately, the watch she wore on her left wrist beeped a certain time.

"I'm afraid I can't do that sir. I have to go," she said and began to head into the inner part of the garden.

"C'mon Lovina we just met and you have to go already? Just come stay with me."

"I will but it has to be some other time. Goodbye Ben," she said and waved at him as she smiled.

"She finally calls me by my name," he muttered to himself with a smile threatening to tear his lips apart. He didn't understand why talking to her or having her call him by his name felt like the best graduation gift ever. He wondered which way it was she had come in from and so decided after much contemplation to go after her. Maybe he would tell him where and when they could have their second meeting. He quickened his steps and before long he was breathing heavily from the little run he did while calling out her name. He got no response as she was long gone but he succeeded in finding out where she had come in from. Behind some cluster of creeping plants was a small door which exited into lonely path. He had not taken notice of that door since he started visiting that garden. He wondered how long she had been visiting the garden to have known every nook and cranny like she did.

"I'll see you sometime soon my lovely garden faerie," he said as he exited the garden with a smile playing at the corners of his lips.

***

Lovina ran as fast as her legs could carry her towards the bakery. Her boss couldn't find out that she had snuck out again unless that would be the end of her stay as a baker in the Bylers' bakery. She couldn't afford losing her job and not seeing Benjamin again for the rest of her life was going to be heart wrecking. She couldn't afford that happening to her. The little pay she got from baking at the Bylers' bakery had been her family's only source of survival. Lovina snuck into the bakery room like nothing had happened and just as she stepped out of the changing room, her boss walked into the kitchen where all the baking was being done. Her friend Sarah glanced at her struggling to knot her apron and smiled.

"You beat the boss today, no more sneaking out alright?" Sarah whispered to her and she nodded. They knew that advice was mostly not always taken as she'd always sneak off to the garden again.

"The Byler's will be visiting the bakery tomorrow for inspection..." The boss, Mrs. Diane Wood announced. "I will want you all to be of very good behavior.

"I will expect nothing less," Loraine mimicked the boss as she waved her hand in the air just the exact same time she was and raised her chin in the air to drive her point home just as the boss always did. Lovina giggled, drawing Diane's attention to herself.

"And what my fair lady could have tickled your fancy so much you couldn't wait for my exit before giggling like a mouse who had just found itself a piece of cheese," she asked as she walked towards Lovina. Lovina looked about her not sure what to say. Diane was gradually losing her patience and she hated being made a mockery of.

"I'm talking to you young lady," she said as she banged her hand on the table before Lovina and sent the flour on the table flying into the air and into her face. She choked on the particles and sneezed so heavily you'd fear an earthquake was about to happen under her robust self. She turned and walked off towards her office with anger.

"We will finish this conversation later you be sure of that young lady, she said as she stomped off. The ladies in the kitchen waited to be sure the door was locked behind her before they all burst out laughing.

"Man, you are the bomb. You gave her just what she wanted," Loraine said and high-fived Lovina.

"Way to go best friend," Sarah said and gave Lovina a hug. Before long the ladies were chattering about the Bylers and how they hoped the young handsome Byler would come with them too. All the ladies practically drooled over him.

"So what did you get me from your lovely garden," Sarah asked Lovina on their way home. Any flowers that I might not know exist already? Lovina smiled at her a twirled as she sighed happily. Sarah knew something was up when she saw her in that mood. Sarah was Lovina's cousin and they were Amish too except that her parents moved to New York City to live due to work. Lovina had come to live with them for the duration of her *rumpspringa* and since she used to work for the Bylers in Lancaster then she decided applying to bake for them wasn't going to be a bad idea as Sarah was working there already. The little money she made was always sent home for the upkeep of her siblings and her parents.

"Lovina? Why are you prancing about like a *kinner* who have just been handed a lollipop? Did something happen in that garden that is a lot better than just gathering flowers?

"He talked to me," Lovina said with a grin a wide as the Atlantic.

"Who talked to you? Wait don't tell me the garden faerie is a male. I'd love to meet him."

"Come off it Sarah .You too? You don't believe in that story do you?

"Well there are a lot of things to believe. The whole garden faerie thing fascinates me and so why wouldn't I believe in it."

"Well, I wasn't talking about any garden faerie. You know I don't believe in that. You know it's just the caretaker's way of scaring *kinner* from tampering with the plants.

"If you weren't talking about the garden faerie then who are you referring to? And why are you flushing bright pink.

"Well I met the Bylers' young handsome boss and he talked to me. He even thought I was the garden faerie as I had lost my prayer *kapp* on my way out to the garden earlier today and so my hair was let down and I stood shielding my face from him as I was crying and bemoaning my *familye's* fate. *Daed* is ill again and the little money I send home isn't helping them. So that thought got me crying and unknown to me, Benjamin was there probably admiring the plants. He heard me crying and came in search of me. He said he wanted to get to know me but my watched beeped alerting that it was time to go and so I left before he could get another word out and to beat Madame Diane's time for afternoon inspection. It seems he was having his graduation party at the park."

"Heard he will be leaving for college real soon. I know you've had a crush on him since he was a little boy and it's a great thing he got to talk to you after all these while. Now does he know you work at his *familye's* bakery?

"*Nee*, he doesn't. But he will by tomorrow," She replied.

"*Gut*. That would be great for you girl. I bet he's already into you. Lovina pondered on what Sarah had said. She really hoped he liked her the way she did him. She only held onto their conversation at the garden like some trophy she had won for the day.

***

Benjamin dressed up and helped the twins into their clothes. They were happy they were going to visit the bakery. They always loved having to go round having a taste of each cake from the kitchen.

The ride to the bakery was an uneventful one. Benjamin wondered when he would see his garden faerie again. He closed his eyes and envisioned her hair falling as low as her waist region. She must have forgotten to wear her prayer *kapp*, he thought. His thoughts lingered on her lips which always found a reason to part into a smile that melted his heart. He smiled in response to the emotion that coursed his body. He was in love with her and he had to find a way to get across to her. He wanted to see her every day; her smile did a lot of things to him. He never believed in love at first sight but if this was what it took to be a victim of love at first sight then he didn't mind being guilty the rest of his life.

The bakery bubbled with activities, ladies sashayed past him and winked at him but he knew his heart was already spoken for. His parents led him into the kitchen where the baking was being done and that was when he spotted her in a corner standing with a bowed head. She looked lovely in her work attire and he was going to let her know. Since his parents were out discussing with Madame Diane, he seized the opportunity to make his move.

"Hey my garden faerie. Now I know why you would rather address me formally but hey, I'd love it if you just called me Ben," he said.

"*Jah*, Si...I mean Ben," Lovina replied flushing bright red.

"Please meet me at the garden today by 16hrs. Would you please do me this huge favor?" he asked taking her hand in his. Lovina's legs melted in a puddle beneath her. Her heart raced like it was in a marathon.

"Hey, look at me," Benjamin said lifting her face gently until her eyes met his.

"Promise me you'll be there."

"I promise," she reassured him. He was overwhelmed with so much happiness that he took her hands to his lips and planting a kiss on both hands bid her farewell.

Evening came as anticipated by both parties and they met at the garden as they had earlier scheduled. They spent their evening walking about the garden and whispering to the plants and pretending they had ears.

"Hey, I'll be leaving for college soon and I want us to start courting before I leave. She turned away from the flower she was admiring to look at him. How could he say he was leaving when they just got together? Was this part of *Gott's* plan too? It felt really frustrating if it was and she wondered why it was so.

He saw the emotion in her eyes. She was hurt by those words and he didn't mean to. He never wished to hurt her but he had to further his studies if ever he wanted to have a comfortable life with the woman he wished to marry.

"I was given a scholarship to study at Bradford School of Business in California and that would take me roughly five years away from you. I'll always visit you and we can always communicate through letters. I wouldn't want to come back and find out you are taken," Benjamin said.

"Ben, this is our first meeting out, we can't just assume we are already in love and rush into things. We can wait until you are done with college and if this lasts until then, then we'll..."

"That is too long a wait, Lovina," Benjamin said taking her hand and drawing her closer to him cutting her short in the process. Lovina's heart skipped two beats in quick succession. She wanted to be with him since she saw him for the first time in the bakery then in their small Amish community in Lancaster County. "I know I can wait for as long as you want me to but what's the wait for when we know what we feel for each other is deeper than we can fathom. C'mon let's get a go at it Love. I don't want to live my whole life blaming myself for not having you to myself when I should have. I know it's too early to say this but I know I love you and would love to be with you." That was all she needed to hear. She took him up in an embrace and that scaled the deal.

The next day the ladies at the bakery were agog with joy for Lovina. They all crowded her table hoping to hear the lovebirds' story from the horse's mouth. She made sure to give them all the juicy part of the story. Being around *Englischers* had thought her to be romantic and know what and what not to tell. She knew what they wanted to hear and she gave it to them the way they wanted it. She just made sure that she was telling the truth.

After they were done for the day, she sat in the changing room and thought over the decision she had made the day before. She wondered if they could ever be together after he was done studying in that reputable Business school. She didn't know where it was but she knew that it was a great distance away when he heard him say he was preparing his flight documents. She was determined to make it work and so she vowed to.

Few days later, she was at the airport to see him off to college alongside his parents.

"Promise you'll wait for me," He said as he was about to board his flight.

"I'll wait for you my love," she said as he planted a kiss on her forehead. The Bylers who knew what was already going on between their son and Lovina knew better than to tell him not to continue with it. He was their first son and throughout his life, he had always obeyed them. Now it was his turn to have something for himself and they weren't going to start now to deny him the things he wanted. He was grown enough to make important decisions like whom to court' for himself. But that wasn't what Lovina's parents wanted to hear. Immediately she was done with her *rumpspringa* she was advised to come home so as she can be picked by one of the single men in the community who were ready to be married.

Lovina had never disobeyed her parents for the first time and she hoped for *Gott's* sake they wouldn't make her to.

"Are you going to court someone else if they asked you to?" Sarah asked as she watched Lovina gather her things together for her journey back home. She knew somehow her parents would allow her come back to the bakery as that was all they had apart from her mother's little quilting business.

"Not in my life I wouldn't. He's everything I wished for Sarah. Everything I prayed for and I cannot let it go because my parents don't want me to wait that long to get married. I know it's difficult but I can't spend the rest of my life with someone I don't love. I'd rather stay unmarried.

"C'mon Love, you don't have to say that. But look at it. It's been three years since he left and his letters have stopped coming. He has also stopped visiting." Lovina walked towards the window and stared into the distance. Sarah was right the last letter she received from him was a year ago and although he had stated that his course of study was taking up all his time, she knew he could still make out time to send her a letter if he wanted to. At first she had been worried to death thinking he was ill or had been involved in one of life's misfortunes but his parents had confirmed that he was alright and that none of such misfortunes befell him. Her thoughts strayed towards the fact that someone somewhere was probably taking his attention away from her and she shook her head vigorously to clear her thoughts. If she started now to have doubts about his loyalty, it will continue all her life and she couldn't afford to let that happen.

"He has been busy and I'm going to trust his words on that. If my parents are so keen to marry one of their *dochders* off then they can have a go at that with my *schweschder.* I'm pretty sure she will succumb to them. I know I have to listen to them and do as they say but I can't have them dictate who I should and shouldn't court. I can wait as long as I want to. It's my life and not theirs." Lovina said as she went back to sit on the bed. She shared a room with her cousin and her two other little cousin shared the room opposite theirs. Her trip back home was for tomorrow so she opted to help out in the kitchen in other to get Benjamin's case off her mind for a while. Somewhere deep down her heart, she was hurting from not having heard from him in a long while.

The next day she wrote to him, hoping he would reply her this time. As she dropped off the letter on her way back to Lancaster County, she prayed *Gott* would remind him of her in some way.

Back home Lovina was welcomed with a special meal of chicken soup and rice. She felt so loved and happy to see her loved once after a long while. Unlike her fellow Amish girls who went for their rumspringa to have fun and frolic about with *Englischers*, she had used her stay to get a job which she loved. She loved working for the Bylers as they were very lovely people. After she was done settling in, her parents called her into their rooms to table the matter they had called her home for.

"Lovina, we'd like for you to get acquainted with the David Graber. You two will make a better couple. You've worked your whole life with the Bylers and we suppose it's high time you move on with your life as a young Amish woman. Lovina couldn't believe her ears. She had hoped her stay at hoem wasn't going to be so frustrating but now it seemed it was the major reason she had been called back home.

"*Mamm, Daed*, you know the money I am paid helps keep this *familye* together in some way. I can't leave the bakery only to come home and get acquainted to some young *mann* that doesn't want to get acquainted to me.

"Well, whether or not he doesn't want to, you will no longer work with them and that is my final say on this issue. While you are home, you can go about making David find you interesting enough to get acquainted to you because believe it or not, that young *mann* who will in no time be sought after by top international organizations will not come back for you. You two are of different worlds and so can never be together. Come to think of it. Where do you even fit in in his top business world?" Lovina stared at her father with tears threatening to erupt from their confines. She was disappointed and at the same time broken hearted. She had earlier thought of these but had hoped it wouldn't turn out to be a problem.

"*Daed*, we are worlds apart but I love him all the same. You can make me stop working for the Bylers but you won't make me stop loving him," she said and stomped of banging the door in her wake. She was annoyed with her parents for suggesting that she forget about Benjamin. What if they her parents had forgotten each other just because of a minor problem, would they have had a family as lovely as the one they have now?

"Lovina," her little brother called tapping her legs which peeked out from under her bed covering. "Please stop crying, he said this time making crying faces. Lovina smiled and spread her arms inviting him to climb the bed. He loved cozying up in her sister's bed. She often teased her other sister who was older than he was and younger than Lovina about it.

"Hey my little prince, do not worry your little head over nothing alright? Your big *schweschder* will be fine, she cooed reassuringly into his ears. He always had a way of making her smile and oh how lovely it was watching him display his love for her. She tickled him and he laughed hysterically.

"What's going on here, Mary asked as she stepped into the room in search of her little brother.

"Come take your little *bruder* away from me or else I'm going to end up dying of laughter," Lovina pelted out from somewhere beneath the covers.

"*Ach*, I'll love to see that happen, Mary said and joined her brother in ticking Lovina. Her siblings were her painkiller and she had no doubt that having them around her could help her get through anything even if it was heartbreak.

***

Benjamin walked into his office and motioned his secretary into the room. He has not been able to return home since his graduation from business school as he was offered a job immediately. He barely had time for anything else apart from the so many meetings he had scheduled with top business clients all over the world. His thoughts a lot of times drifted to Lovina but he always hoped that somehow his absence and silence wouldn't make her change her mind.

"Do I have any letters from anyone, Lovina maybe?" He asked.

"Sir Lovina's letters stopped coming a long time ago. But you have a letter from one Sarah, she said fidgeting with the stack of papers she had in her hand until she found the envelope she was looking for.

Benjamin's brows furrowed. That was new, Sarah never wrote to him and how could he have been so busy not to notice that Lovina's letters were no longer coming? Had something happened to Lovina all these while and he had failed to notice due to work? All these thoughts and more assailed his mind as he ripped open the envelope to read the letter from Sarah. It was dated some weeks ago. The letter said that Lovina had been worried so much that she fell ill and wouldn't eat unless she saw he was alright. The letter admonished him for having abandoned Lovina for his business world. It told him of Lovina's doubt of his love and this broke his heart. It was his fault that lovina was ill. He turned to his secretary with all the pent up emotion the letter had roused in him.

"This letter came in three weeks ago and you kept it from me? What were you even thinking?"

"Sir, I couldn't have gotten it across to you since you were on a business trip. Moreover, you instructed that I keep the unofficial mails for later."

"Not these ones Emily not these ones," he lamented slamming his hands on his table. Go book me the next flight to New York. I have to go see Lovina, he ordered. The confused secretary looked at him like he had grown two horns at that moment.

"Right now?"

"Off course right now," he replied and turned towards his window resting his head on the glass pane. He prayed that Lovina was alright and would forgive him for leaving her in the dark. He had been a terrible partner and he hoped to change. He couldn't afford to lose her.

"But Sir you have a business meeting in the next few min..." his secretary began to say.

"Damn, the business meeting woman. I'm going home. Now go get me my flight ticket," he shouted sending his secretary flying right out the door to her laptop.

***

As the flight made its way into the sky, Benjamin decided he was done causing his heartthrob much hurt. He was going to ask her to marry him. As his flight landed at the airport in New York City, he made a silent prayer to *Gott* to heal her heart of the hurt he had caused her so she would agree to what he had in mind. He told *Gott* that if it was part of his plan that he should make her forgive him even before he got to set his eyes on her. he took a cab from the airport straight to the bakery and as he got down from the cab, he tipped him to wait out there for him while he took care of a pressing issue.

Rushing through the swinging doors he headed for the kitchen apologizing to everybody he ran into. The staff wondered why their boss was in such haste, they had never seen him in so much hurry before well, they barely saw him at all. He spotted Sarah walking down the hall away from the kitchen. She was finished for the day and was about leaving.

"Sarah? Wait up Sarah," he called as he made his way towards her. Sarah stopped in her tracks when she noticed who it was.

"Tired of touring the world already? Well I bet there are even more countries you haven't visited. What do you want? A map to more hearts you can break?" She asked sarcasm and annoyance practically drooling from her voice.

"Forgive me Sarah, I've been stupid and I know I shouldn't have taken this long to get back."

"The one person you should be throwing these words at is no longer here. If it can take you three good weeks to look at letter that says Lovina is critically ill and is asking for you, then maybe you do not deserve her and she should probably move on with her life, which she must have as waiting all these while and not hearing from you have taken its toll on her," Sarah said and made to leave.

"Please take me to her Sarah. I can't afford to live without her."

"How many years did it take you to realize you can't do without her?"

"C'mon Sarah please," he pleaded.

"Fine, I'll take you there. Luckily for them the company's cab was in good shape so retrieving his things from the airport taxi, he hit the engine of the cab and let his human compass guide him to his garden faerie.

****

Lovina who still craved for Benjamin sat beside her mum and questioned her if *Gott's* plan was really a thing or just an excuse to run away from the obvious.

"Lovina, you have to understand that a lot of times *Gott* does things for our own *gut*. Benjamin might not have been the best *mann* for you. He probably might not be the one," her mother replied.

"But *mamm*, I can't love anyone else. I can't believe he abandoned me. When the letters stopped coming I thought he had just been really busy but how could he not even try to reach out for four years now. I really wish I guarded my heart from falling in love with him. Now I can't go back and my heart can't stop breaking into tiny shards each time he comes to my mind," She said as tears rolled down her cheeks. She clenched her heart which seemed to resonate with so much hurt. Just then she spotted the Bylers' company cab from afar and smiled. Sarah always visited her in that cab since she didn't have a cab. She always looked forward to seeing her as she gave her the zeal to move on with life. She sat up and waited for the car to pullover in front of the house. Looking closely, she saw that the cab wasn't being driven by Sarah. Who could the other person be? Did she have to bring a staff this time to teach me how to move on? The cab finally came to a stop and out came the least person she expected to see. Lovina stood transfixed and watched as Benjamin made his way towards her. At that moment the earth seemed to be rotating in the opposite direction as she wondered if she had suddenly found herself in some other country.

"Lovina, I am sorry for everything." Benjamin began to say. Lovina was tired of crying as she stood there dried eyed and staring at Benjamin like he had fallen from a different planet altogether.

"It wasn't supposed to happen like this. I really didn't mean to ignore your letters and the different other ways in which you tried to reach out to me. I am really sorry

Love. I have no tangible excuse for keeping you in the dark all these while. Please forgive me,"

"Ben, I understand quite well that I don't fit into your corporate world. You could have found a better way to tell me that our worlds are so far apart that nothing can bring them together again. Not even love can," Lovina said staring at him defiantly.

"How do you mean my love?" Benjamin asked oblivious of what she was trying to say.

"Sarah, let's go in now, my siblings can wait to see you. They've been longing to have you around," Lovina said turning to Sarah and ignoring him. Sarah was surprised. She would have approved of this behavior if he hadn't pleaded with her to bring him to her.

"Lovina, I think you should hear him out. He's being sincere and I know it because I saw that look in his eyes. I have never seen it in a guy's eyes in a long while now,"

"I can't believe you're taking sides with him," Lovina said staring at Sarah with unbelief and anger clouding her judgment. Benjamin walked up to her teary eyed. He knelt before her and pleaded.

He didn't mind. He was going to do anything at all to get her to forgive him. "Please forgive me my love. I never meant to hurt you. I was carried away by so much work. I always had a busy schedule. He wasn't about to start telling her that the reason behind his work crammed schedule was because he was one of the best international business moguls. That to him felt like gloating and he knew it wouldn't get him anywhere.

Lovina hated seeing him this broken. It hurt her that he was shedding tears. She brought her hands to his cheeks and wiped his tears.

"Please rise, I can't stand your tears. You are forgiven, just don't cry anymore," she said embracing him and crying at the same time.

"Hey, ssssh. No more crying okay?" Benjamin said. He looked into those brown orbs of hers and asked her to be his wife.

"My lovely garden faerie please say you will be mine, now and forever," he said boring her eyes with the expectation radiating from his.

Lovina smiled and taking his hands in hers reassured him. "I'll always be your garden faerie my love."

THE END...

AMISH & WIDOWED

ABBY BARKER

BOOK ONE

Eve looked wistfully out the window of the moving cab as it flew through the Pennsylvania countryside. She began to recognize some of the seemingly immortal farmhouses that still stood in the barley fields she remembered from her childhood. Field after field rolled by interspersed with herds of cattle and the odd corner store. She felt a small ball of nerves form in her abdomen. It had been years since she had been back home. Sarah, Isaac, and Aaron came to visit her every once in a while, but Eve hadn't returned the favor since her daughter's wedding. Now that her husband had passed, she started to become lonely. She could only distract herself for so long with knitting, even if the bag of handmade hats and gloves in the trunk said otherwise.

The taxi driver looked back in his rearview mirror and noticed her looking pensively out the window.

"Are you alright, ma'am?"

"Oh, yes, thank you. I'm just remembering the last time I was here. On the outside, nothing much has changed, but it feels so different to me. I must sound like a crazy old lady!"

"Not at all, ma'am. I always feel that way when I visit my parents back home. Must be the person that changes more than the place."

"Must be," Eve replied. She thought it might be rude to tell him that she didn't feel all that different either. She could easily imagine herself as she was now playing in the yard of her family's house, sitting on her mother's lap as she read her story, or walking to town to pick up supplies to bake her husband a birthday cake. Even though her appearance had been altered so drastically over the years, her insides felt more or less unchanged. Although it might look silly from an outsider's perspective to see an old woman toddling around in a child's jumper, reaching out to her father to swing her around, in Eve's imagination it seemed totally natural, at least in this context. She laughed at the idea of wearing diapers again. That was something that could actually become a reality at her age. *What a full circle that would be,* she thought.

The pair drove through the countryside for a few miles more before finally making a turn off the main road. The homes started to get closer together and streets were filled with more and more people. Mothers in bonnets wrangled their children and fathers tended to the yard work and livestock. She watched neighbors greet each other reliable horse and buggy drivers smile and wave as they passed one another. They were all familiar sights, but after being away for so long it was almost jarring to see. The small town she and her husband lived in was by no means a bustling city, but it was not nearly as personal and welcoming as her old Amish home. At least, it would be if she didn't feel like such an outsider after all this time.

Even though the community was lax on rules regarding leaving and excommunication, she still worried that her reception here might not be the friendliest. She had no reason to believe this other than her own anxieties, she hadn't even said as much as "hello" to anyone but the taxi driver yet, but she still couldn't shake the worry. Nerves cinched her stomach as they approached the one-story white farmhouse that she knew so well. There was not much that set it apart from its neighbors, but Eve recognized it right away. It may have been the crooked shutter on the kitchen window that no one ever got around to fixing, or the towering old oak that's shaded the home for as long as she could remember, or maybe it was just the instincts of an old woman. In any case, she knew it immediately.

"Thanks, dear. This will do just fine."

"No problem, ma'am. I hope you find things exactly as you left them."

I hope I don't, she thought to herself, but smiled outwardly at the driver and paid him his fare. She didn't have much luggage, so she refused his offer to help her carry it inside. She was old, but not frail. She paused at the front door, paint chipped across the front. She hoped this wasn't symbolic of what was inside, but then chastised herself for being dramatic. Eve took a deep breath and knocked on the door.

Footsteps approached from inside, the door swung open, and Eve was immediately swept up into a warm hug.

"Mama! I'm so happy to see you. It's been too long. Too, too long! Isaac, come help Mama with her things."

"Oh, don't bother with that, Sarah. I'm perfectly capable of carrying my own bags."

"I know you are, you stubborn woman. Let us play the part of hosts, and you the part of fragile old grandmother, won't you? Just this once?" Sarah asked with a wink.

"Just this once, darling," Eve responded, begrudgingly handing over her possessions to Isaac who just appeared in the doorway.

"Mrs. Fisher! Welcome. Allow me."

"Mrs. Fisher? Bah. Isaac, you've been married to my daughter for seventeen years. If you're not going to call me Mama at least call me Eve. 'Mrs. Fisher' makes me feel old." It also reminded her of her deceased husband, but she didn't feel the need to dampen the joyous reunion with her dark feelings.

"Alright, Eve, I'll drop the formalities. Can I show you to your room?"

"That would be lovely, but just so I know which one it is. I've been sitting in silence for so long, I'd love to have a nice chat over a cup of tea."

"That can be arranged, Mama. I'll put a kettle on while you get settled. Aaron and Beth went into town to pick up some things for dinner, but he should be back soon. Those children have been missing their Nana something fierce."

"Oh, I'm sure a couple of teenagers have better things to do than hang out with their grandmother, but I'm excited to see them, nonetheless."

Eve followed Isaac to the end of the long hall off the kitchen to the master bedroom, her old room. She assumed that the couple would remain in that room and was surprised when he dropped her bags at the foot of the bed.

"Isaac, you and your wife should have this room. This is a room for a married couple, not a visiting widow. I'd be happy to sleep in a broom closet."

"Don't be silly. This was your home first. It wouldn't feel right to put you in the guest room. Sarah and I will be perfectly fine in there."

"If you insist. Thank you, Isaac."

Eve tried to mask the hesitation in her voice. It would be too difficult to explain that she had never spent a night in this room without her husband. Even at her current home, she started sleeping on the couch after he died. Her back had suffered, but she just couldn't bring herself to slip under the covers when she knew he wouldn't be there waiting for her. She hoped that it had been long enough since they shared this particular bed that she'd be able to get a good night's sleep.

"No problem, Eve. Go ahead and unpack. Meet us in the kitchen once you're ready."

The dresser had been emptied to make room for her things. Eve tried not to watch herself as she folded each item of clothing and placed them carefully inside, but she couldn't avoid it. Her thin, grey hair was pinned neatly into a bun behind her head. Small wisps framed her face, wrinkled but by years of smiles and laughter. Her icy blue eyes always look filled with tears, no matter her mood. She wished she could change that, dry them out. To be reminded of sadness every time she looked at herself was frustrating, at best, and painful, at worst.

Eve threw a scarf over the mirror and finished unpacking. She wasn't going to let something as silly as her own reflection spoil her family reunion. After all of her clothes had been neatly folded and the bag of knitting ready to distribute, she finished by placing her worn out diary next to the bed. It was the same exact diary that she kept on that very nightstand so many years ago. It looked almost as if it had never left, but it's faded cover and its filled pages gave it away. Eve had spent years filling that book with words of wisdom, day-to-day musings, and the odd doodle. There were still a handful of empty pages left that she was anxious to fill; an entire marriage's worth of information, and then some.

She didn't take the time to notice it before, but as she made her way back down the hall to the kitchen she saw a new set of photographs hanging on the wall. Between what was the guest room and Aaron's room hung a family portrait from Sarah and Isaac's wedding. Sarah stood, glowing, in the center with Isaac at her side. Seventeen years and she hadn't aged a day. Isaac wasn't looking too bad either. On Sarah's right arm, Eve saw herself, and behind her was Eddie. The photo perfectly captured his lively eyes, which were looking straight at his daughter instead of the lens. She remembered looking through the pictures from that day with Sarah and noticing that he never once took his eyes off of her and that proud smile never left his face.

That's how she'd always like to remember him. Standing tall at his daughter's wedding, not pale and bedridden on his last days. She felt the familiar pain begin to wash over her, but shoved it back down. It had been almost six months since he passed. She should be able to think about him without breaking down by now. She took one last look at the idyllic scene frozen in that moment before continuing onto the kitchen. She'd have to get used to passing it everyday.

A pot of steaming tea greeted Eve when she walked into the kitchen. Sarah stirred sugar into her cup at the table while Isaac put together a small tray of cookies, crackers and other teatime snacks.

"How nice to see a husband do some of the kitchen work while his wife relaxes."

Sarah laughed, "Things are a little different around here than when you and Papa got married. Sometimes he even wears my apron!"

"That's true," Isaac chuckled, "it makes me feel pretty."

"Your father would never go so far as to hold my apron. He was a great man, but old fashioned until the day he died."

Eve immediately regretted using that word. A stifling tension came over the two women. Isaac noticed it immediately and stepped in to clear the air.

"But even I'm not ready to wear your bonnet, Sarah."

The trio laughed nervously and tried to let the tension slide off, but they couldn't avoid the subject forever and Sarah thought it better to jump over that hurdle sooner rather than later.

"How are you doing, Mama? How have you been since...you know."

The question Eve was dreading, but expecting.

"I'm fine, love. Really." She wasn't ready to answer it, but Sarah pushed her.

"Mama, I know you're not fine. You and Papa were married for forty-eight years. You don't just forget a relationship like that overnight."

"I haven't forgotten. Believe me, I haven't forgotten, but I'm telling you that I'm fine."

"Mama..."

"Sarah, I'm fine. How many times do I have to say it?"

Isaac clearly wanted to step in, but knew better than to get in between his wife and his mother-in-law. They shared the same stubbornness that he knew would get him into trouble if he tried. Instead, he quietly filled their cups with more hot water while the two of them fumed. Eventually, Sarah relented. She had fewer years of practice than her mother.

"I miss him, too, you know."

"I know, sweetheart. I know."

They sat at the table, somberly sipping their tea for a while before anyone spoke again. The conversation stayed light, but tense, until Aaron and Beth walked through the door, relieving everyone in the room.

"Nana! You made it."

Aaron towered over his grandmother as he leaned down to embrace her. His sandy blonde hair was disheveled and he had grown taller than his father. She almost didn't recognize the little boy she remembered from their last visit, but his contagious smile, so like Eddie's, was unmistakable. This bubbly teenager couldn't be anyone else but her grandson. Almost completely obscured by her older brother, Beth's lithe frame followed shortly behind him. Less boisterous and more reserved than Aaron, Sarah often referred to her daughter as a "quiet, little observer." Beth was the undoubtedly the most intelligent of all the Millers, but she almost never gave anyone a chance to see it. Sometimes Isaac would silently walk past her open bedroom door to sneak a peek at Beth reading on her bed. It was then that she look her happiest.

"Aaron, you're so tall! How do you even fit through the doorway anymore? Your father's going to have to widen all of these frames for you soon if you don't stop growing. And my darling Beth, you look even more angelic than the last time I saw you."

Beth just smiled widely and hugged her grandmother. Eve did not expect any more enthusiasm from the blonde introvert.

"Well, I'll be able to help him out when he does. I've been apprenticing to be a carpenter with Mr. Miller on the other side of town. I made the chair you're sitting in!"

"Look at that! And it only wobbles a little," Eve joked.

"It does not. Does it?"

Aaron grabbed the back of the chair and moved it around a little, worried that she was right, but the chair didn't wiggle an inch.

"You got me, Nan. I forgot about your ruthless sense of humor."

"That's me! Ruthless old Nana."

"Hey, I never said anything about 'old.' You don't look a day over twenty-five to me."

"And what would that make me," Sarah chimed in, "a toddler?"

"I can't be married to a two-year-old, Aaron. It's just not right."

This made the family burst out into their first genuine laugh since Eve arrived. It was a relief to them all to know that they could still talk and tease so naturally after the funeral. That was the last time they had all seen each other, and there was not any laughter then. It felt good to relax and let go a little, but once she did, Eve realized how tired traveling had made her.

"I didn't feel it up until now, but I'm actually quite tired. I think I'll take a short nap before supper time."

"Of course, Mama. Lay down for a while and we'll get started on the meal." Sarah reached across the table to grab her mother's hand. Eve gave hers a squeeze in return.

"Thanks, sweetheart. I can't tell you how happy I am to see you all. Please, excuse me. I'll be rested at dinner."

"I'm glad you're here, Nan."

As she passed by the family photo hanging in the hall again, she noticed it didn't make her feel as sad before. Before she went to sleep that night, she wrote a few words about the importance of family.

***

Eve awoke to the smells of cooking meat and brewing coffee. They'd prepared a big welcome meal for her. *Completely unnecessary,* she thought, but she realized she was starving. Eve dressed for supper and met the family in the kitchen, as well as a handful of neighbors that she didn't expect.

"Surprise!" yelled Sarah from the stove when she noticed her mother in the doorway. "You have some visitors here to see you."

That's when Eve started to recognize some of the faces around the table. These ghosts took her aback from her past. The older couple was friends of her and Eddie's. Years ago, when they lived in this house, Ernest and Harriet Gingerich were their best friends. On Saturday evenings, they would alternate hosting potlucks and Dutch Blitz nights at each other's homes. They'd mostly gab about church or what outlandish thing the Grabers had done that day. When she and Eddie moved away, they all lost touch. It's not easy to get a hold of the Amish from 1,000 miles away.

The lanky brunette cradling a toddler was Ernest and Harriet's son, Benjamin. Eve assumed the child was his, even though she had a difficult time wrapping her head around that. The last time she saw Benjamin he was a child himself. The woman beside him was unmistakably the child's mother, and Benjamin's wife. She pushed her dark hair behind her ears as she leaned down to coo at the little girl in her husband's lap. Benjamin and his wife shared a smile that left no question as to their relationship. So much had changed over the years, but these were still the people she knew.

"Harriet and Ernest! Benjamin, I haven't seen you since you were just a boy. And who are these two lovely creatures?"

"Aunt Eve, meet my wife Delilah and my daughter Gracie."

The wide-eyed little girl looked over at Eve and flashed an enormous grin. One pudgy hand pulled at her bouncy set of curly locks while the other opened and closed in a wave.

"Hiya! Gracie!"

Benjamin and Delilah laughed.

"No, you're Gracie! That's Auntie Eve."

"Gracie! Hiya, Auntie Ebe!"

"She's just learning to form full sentences. Gracie's quite the chatterbox, even if she's not always exactly right," Delilah offered with a soft smile.

"Oh, she'll learn, no doubt. I remember when Benji was that age. He had much less interest in talking than he had in throwing stones at my ankles. You were trouble, young man!"

"My, Benjamin at two years old. It's hard to imagine that handsome jaw on a little boy. But the stone throwing, that I can see."

Delilah winked at her husband and he feigned embarrassment. Eve felt a pang of jealousy seeing the love between the two young people. When she and Eddie first started going steady, he would take her out for rides in his family's buggy. They told their parents they were going to the corner store, but they really didn't have a destination in mind. They pair would drive around for hours, talking about their childhoods their futures, what they had for breakfast and what they wanted to have for supper. She could talk about anything with Eddie and it felt like the most interesting conversation in the world. When they'd finally stop to give the horses a rest, she'd tease him about pulling the buggy himself.

"Maybe it's time you pull your weight around here, and mine!" she'd say and he'd give her the same look Benji gave Delilah at the supper table. She had to look away to keep from crying.

"Earnest, Harriet, it's been, what, seventeen years since I've seen you two? It had to have been the wedding! Still selling candles, Harrie?"

"From time to time. Things have slowed down a bit now that we've reached this ripe old age of a million. Now I just make them for fun, despite Ernie's protests."

"What's there to protest? There's nothing wrong with having a hobby."

"You should see our house, filled to the brim with candles! Then you might change your tune," Ernie interjected.

"He's afraid I'm going to burn the house down. It's not like I light them all at once!"

"It doesn't matter if there's only one candle lit, you knock that one over and the rest go up in flames. The whole house is a fire hazard."

"Psh. You worry too much, dear. It's not like I'm dancing through the halls waving my arms."

"Well, what if I wanted to dance? I couldn't, could I?"

"Earnest Gingerich when have you ever felt the urge to dance?"

"I'm not saying I have. I'm just saying I might."

Harriet sighed a defeated sigh.

"It looks like I need to get rid of some candles to support my husband's newfound love of dance, Eve. Would you like to buy some candles?"

The entire kitchen filled with laughter, something Eve dearly missed about this place. At home, she'd have the odd guest for dinner, or a neighbor might stop by after work to ask her for a favor, but three generations under one roof was something special. When she left the community, she knew the benefits – technology, modern comforts, a more lucrative job for Eddie – but she didn't think about what she might be leaving behind. Aaron was only sixteen, but she wondered when he might have children of his own. She wanted to see her family grow before it was her turn to pass. The least she could do was tell Eddie how sweet his grandchildren were when she got there. *Again with this unceasing morbidity,* she chastised herself.

"Delilah, dear, are you from here? Do I know your parents?"

"Oh, no, ma'am..."

"Eve, please. None of this "ma'am" nonsense. You'll make me feel old!"

"Eve. I grew up in an English town nearby, actually."

"Oh! So you weren't raised Amish, then?"

"No, ma'am, I mean Eve, sorry."

Eve smiled kindly. She could tell the young woman felt nervous about disclosing her background. She probably hadn't received the warmest reception from some of the families in town. There's was a progressive community, for the most part. Amish converts were uncommon, but not unheard of, and usually welcomed with open arms. Some families, however, were hard-and-fast traditionalists who wouldn't so much as acknowledge a former outsider, no matter how devote. Eve and her family fell in the first category. Why punish a person for something as uncontrollable as how they were born?

"I was raised Mennonite, but after meeting Benji I decided to convert. I fell in love with being Amish just as much as I fell in love with him."

"That's beautiful, Delilah. I love to see people convert to Amish; it means they've chosen to be here. I don't think it happens enough, honestly."

Eve saw a wave of relief wash over Delilah in the form of a genuine smile. She really was a beautiful girl, but it was the kind of beauty one could overlook if they weren't paying attention. When she smiled, though, there was no mistaking it.

"How did the two of you meet? It's not everyday the English and the Amish are in the same place."

"Well, Benji's buggy had broken a wheel on the main road and my father and I happened to drive by at the time. I insisted we stop and help. I knew my father could fix a car so I was sure he could fix a buggy, but I was wrong. Carpentry and mechanics have some overlap but they're not exactly the same, it turns out. Anyway, we stop and my father does his best, but to no avail. We end up giving him a ride back into to town so he can recruit some people who actually can help him. We talked a bit in the car and, well I don't believe in love at first sight, but I knew I wanted to see him again. I was pretty sure he felt the same way so I decided right then just to tell him how I felt, but he beat me to it. When my father stepped out of the car to talk to Earnest, Benji turned right around and asked me to meet him once he fixed his buggy."

"The rest is history, and the long, painful process of convincing our parents this wasn't a terrible idea."

"Don't be mistaken, we loved Delilah from the very beginning. It was our Benjamin who was trouble, sweeping a young English girl off her feet and stealing her away to an Amish lifestyle."

"True love knows no religion, Ma, and luckily she didn't realize I threw stones as a child until after we were married!"

Their laughter was only interrupted by Isaac putting food on the table. The spread included an array of grains and vegetables, hearty pork chops, and chunks of crusty bread. Eve couldn't be happier for the traditional Amish meal in front of her. A taste of home. The families joined hands for a silent prayer. Eve thought about the dinners she and Eddie used to have, just she and him. They'd pray, holding each other's hands across the corner of the table, never saying a word but sometimes he'd squeeze her hands and she'd squeeze back, sometimes rhythmically and they'd both giggle. Sometimes he'd say, "I prayed for a million more days with you," and her heart would swell before he'd follow that with, "and a million chickens so we'll never go hungry or to sleep!" and they'd laugh again.

Every moment with Eddie was filled with joy, from silent prayer to those private moments in bed together when they should have been silent and asleep but couldn't be. She wasn't even necessarily thinking about the times they were physically intimate, although those memories were just as special, but those nights when they just had to keep talking to each other. They'd share secrets they just couldn't keep in any longer, or tell each other about the day they had even though they'd been together for its entirety. There were evenings when they'd just whisper the thoughts that popped into their heads, just to keep talking. Eddie was her best friend for forty-eight years and then some. She prayed that she'd see him again some day.

Eve squeezed the hands on either side of her when the prayer ended, for good measure. The families dug into the meal, passing platters around the table and pouring each other water and coffee. No one went without that supper. They ate until their bellies were full of food and hearts were full of each other's presence. They made small talk and reminisced about old times over the meal. Nobody brought up Eddie until desert. Benjamin had been talking about the time he let Gracie help him feed the goats and one nibbled on her little finger when Aaron chimed in with a story of his own.

"That's just like the time Grandpa let me help him clean out the barn. I had a rake taller than me and was trying to move the hay into a pile, but I was only making a bigger mess. I had gotten too close to a horse and he nipped me by the back of the collar and tossed me to the floor. I started to cry and Grandpa rushed over. When he realized I was more frightened than hurt, he started to laugh and said, 'You were supposed to move the hay, not be the hay, boy!' To this day, I can't go near a horse without a healthy suspicion."

There were a couple polite nods in response from the Gingriches, but the Millers stayed silent. Aaron was not having any of it.

"Ma, Pa, we've got to be able to talk about Grandpa Eddie without clamming up. It's been six months and I know the sadness isn't all gone, it probably never will be, and I feel it too, but I want to be able to talk about the good stuff without feeling guilty. What's the point of ever having known him if we can't remember him?"

The Gingriches and Isaac were silent, but Sarah looked like she was on the verge of tears. Beth watched inquisitively, but her face did not give away what she might be feeling. Eve spoke up.

"Aaron, did I ever tell you about how your Grandpa Eddie and I met?"

Aaron's looked at her with his teary eyes and smiled.

"No, I don't think I've heard that story."

"Well, unsurprisingly it was at a Sunday singing. We sat across the table from one another and did our best to avoid eye contact for the entire night. You know how it goes. He would stare at me when he thought I wasn't looking and the second I glanced back at him his eyes would dart away, and I would do the same. This went on for several weeks. We'd always find a way to sit near each other, but we never once spoke. I was too shy, and who knows what was going on in his head. Eventually, after all of these mind games, he turned to me one night after the sing and said, 'Hop in my buggy.' Just like that! I knew the man for forty years, but some things will always stay a mystery to me. Against my better judgment, I did hop into his buggy and the whole way home we chatted as if all those stolen glances were actually full-fledged conversations. He was an odd bird, but I was smitten ever since. Now that I think about it, it's not all that interesting of a story! Sorry to blather on like a senile old lady."

"No, Mama. It was beautiful. I'd never heard the whole story before, but that sounds just like Papa. He always had something on his mind that he wouldn't share with anyone else. You could see it twinkling in his eyes."

"I guess I'd never thought to share it because of how unremarkable I thought it to be. Knowing what I know now, though, how could any story about two people falling in love be unremarkable?"

Sarah was openly crying now. She got out of her chair and walked over to her mother. Kneeling down in front of her, she threw her head in Eve's lap and wrapped her arms around her waist.

"I love you, Mama."

"I love you, too, Sarah. Your father loved you so much. I know I haven't been a great example of this, but I know he wouldn't want you to dwell on his passing. He wouldn't want that for any of us. Aaron's right. We have to look back on his life with joy, not on his death with sadness. I have to set an example if I want it to be followed. I loved Eddie, I still love him, but it does me no good to let this pain mar what time I've got left with the other people I love who are still here. You were right, too, sweetheart. I can't pretend like your father never existed. It isn't fair to him and it isn't fair to any of us."

Eve brushed the hair back from her daughter's face and wiped away her tears. She held Sarah's head in her hands and left a gentle kiss in the center of her forehead. She then rapidly blinked her eyes as if waking up from a dream.

"Oh my, things certainly took a turn there for a moment. Ernie, Harrie, Benji and Delilah, my apologies for putting such a damper on what was turning out to be a lovely reunion. Let's get you more pie, hmm?"

"Please, Eve, don't apologize! I know we hadn't seen you or Eddie for a very long time, but we still considered him a lifelong friend, you as well. Never apologize for mourning or remembering a loved one. Excuse me if I'm speaking for everyone here, but I believe we all benefitted from hearing about Eddie."

The rest of the Gingriches nodded in agreement with Earnest's sentiments.

'Thank you, all, for being so understanding. Our family has been through a lot as of late, and we haven't had much time to process it all together. We're lucky to have friends like you to stand by us."

Everyone around the table raised a glass to Isaac's toast, with the exception of Gracie who grabbed at her father's cup as he raised it into the air.

"Cheers! Good health and happiness to us all!"

****

Eve woke up just before sunrise the next morning. Sarah and Isaac were still sleeping, but they'd be up soon. Aaron had a free day and liked to sleep in so there was no telling when she'd see him next. Beth's room was already empty. She was most likely out enjoying a quite sunrise walk to herself. Out on the porch, she watched the sunrise from a rocking chair. A handful of neighbors were already out and about, starting the morning's chores, tending to their animals, and some watching the sun rise just as she was. The street bustled, but it was quiet in the cool morning air. She didn't mind having this moment to herself just to observe the world unfold around her, but was pleasantly surprised when Aaron sat down in the chair next to her.

"Good morning, Nan. Did you sleep well?"

"I did, yes. It was a comfort to sleep in such a familiar room. I didn't realize how much I missed it."

"I'm glad."

Aaron paused with enough intention that Eve knew he had something else on the tip of his tongue.

"Something on your mind, Aaron?"

"I just want to thank you for talking about Grandpa Eddie yesterday. Ma and Pa have refused to say a word about him since he passed and it's been torture. If I so much as say the word "grand" Ma flinches. And Pa just tells me not to upset Ma. I've wanted to talk to you something fierce, Nan, but it's not so easy when you don't have a phone or a computer."

Eve felt a pang of guilt. She should have come back sooner to visit her grieving family. It was selfish of her to have stayed away for so long without so much as a letter. She thought what she was doing would be best for her. It would have been too painful to come back to a place filled with so many memories of Eddie. She didn't once think about whether or not her family might need her.

"Aaron...I'm so sorry, dear. I didn't realize how selfish I was being by not coming home."

"Oh, Nan, that's not what I meant at all! You were right to take all the time you needed to mourn Grandpa Eddie. I've never been in love like that, but I can't imagine losing it once I've got it. It takes a strong person to get over something like that all on their own."

Eve was blown away by her sixteen-year-old grandson's penchant for empathy. She couldn't remember ever meeting a teenaged boy with such a high level of emotional intelligence, with the exception of Eddie. There was no doubt that he was his grandfather's descendant. Even with his reassurance, she still couldn't shake the idea that he had to go through this all by himself. She wished Sarah would have been more open with him, but, then again, Eve hadn't been that way with her own daughter. Aaron noticed her furrowed brow.

"You're here now and that's all that matters. I know Ma's happy to see you, and Pa. They should be getting up soon, but I'm sure the pigs are wondering where their breakfast is. I'd better go feed them."

"Hold on a second, dear. I want to give you something."

Eve had been holding on to Eddie's old pocket watch since his passing. It had stopped ticking long before he had died. Eddie said he kept carrying it with him as a good luck charm. He told her, "A stopped clock is still right twice a day. If I could ever be so lucky!" She nagged him to get it fixed but he refused. When she inherited it the urge to repair it disappeared. The watch didn't feel inherently lucky to her, but somewhere in her mind she worried that if she did fix it, it would become unlucky. Eve liked carrying a piece of him around with her, but the superstition it came with weighed on her unnecessarily. It wouldn't bother Aaron, though, and he might even fix the watch and make it useful again. That was one difference between Aaron and Eddie, probably for the better.

She had put the pocket watch in the top, left side drawer of the wardrobe where Eddie used to keep his socks. Eddie was a very conservative dresser, except for his socks. He'd wander around the house in sharp grey slacks and a crisp white shirt but every once in a while he'd tap her on the shoulder and whisper, "look," as if it were a secret just for her, and lift up his pant leg. Some days a happy little dog would look up at her from his ankle, other days it would be a serene sailboat, or gaudy rainbow. He'd laugh to himself and go on with his day, reveling in the fact that only they knew that under his put together shell he had a delightful surprise underneath. They buried him in a pair covered in wildflowers.

Eve found the watch right where she left it, still broken, still lucky. The weight of it felt heavier than usual in her palm as she carried it outside. This was the last physical thing that she had of Eddie's and it was hard to let go of, but she knew she didn't need it. Eddie was not inside the pocket watch and keeping it with her didn't bring him closer.

Remembering Eddie brought him as close as he was going to get. She had to learn to be okay with that. She didn't need the pocket watch, but Aaron did.

"Here," she said to him, handing over the small golden circle, "this was Grandpa Eddie's."

Aaron clicked a button on the side and popped open the watch's cover to reveal the mother-of-pearl face underneath.

"It's broken! It must have stopped working after Grandpa died."

"It must have." He didn't need to know about Eddie's silly superstitions. That boy would go on carrying around a broken watch until the day he died if he knew. But if she kept it from him, he'd fix it and bring new life to the watch. Eve want him to inherit something practical from his grandfather.

"I'll tinker around with it and fix it. Thanks, Nan. You don't know how much this means to me."

Not as much as if I was here for you when you needed me, she thought. Giving him the pocket watch was the very least she could do.

"Your grandfather would have wanted you to have it. You'd never find him without that thing."

"You won't catch me without it either. I think I have a tiny tool set around here somewhere. Let me go find it."

Aaron quickly hugged his grandmother and quickly bounded away. He was a "fixer" and nothing brought him more joy than a new project.

The sun had fully risen now and more people were in their yards starting on their chores. Eve's back was not as strong as it used to be and arthritis was beginning to touch her joints so she wouldn't be much use doing heavy labor, but she was still determined to help out while she was here. Even though it had been so many years it was hard to shake the feeling that this was her home. She walked back into the house and decided to get to work making breakfast.

Eve hadn't cooked for more than just herself in some time. She had gotten into the habit of cutting her favorite recipes in half. Despite having to put less effort into making a meal, cooking for one was not easier. Eve shuffled through the pantry collecting spices, grains, fruits and vegetables; everything she needed to create a spectacular breakfast for her family. She wanted to say "thank you" for being such gracious hosts, but more than that she wanted to say "I'm sorry" for taking so long to get there. She'd never be able to say it with words, but she thought I nice hearty meal might do the trick. She was almost finished cooking when Sarah and Isaac finally emerged from their room.

"What is that amazing smell?" Isaac asked, finishing his question with a huge yawn. "We probably would have never gotten out of bed without something so enticing beckoning us down the hall."

"I just thought I'd cook up a little something to show you how much appreciate your hospitality. It's the very least that I could do."

"It's no problem at all, Mama. I can't tell you how happy we are to have you here."

Sarah was smiling, but the bags under her eyes seemed to give away the fact that she didn't get much sleep.

"No wonder you two slept in so long. You look exhausted."

"After what happened at dinner last night, Isaac and I stayed up talking for a while. I realized that there were some things I was bottling up since Papa died."

"It's important that a husband and wife have strong communication between them. I understand why you wouldn't want to talk to me, but I'm surprised you kept anything from Isaac. And Isaac, can't you tell when your wife's upset by now?"

Sarah was taken aback by her mother's accusatory tone. She respected Eve's opinion, but couldn't understand why she was accusing Isaac of not being an attentive husband.

"Of course Isaac could tell I was upset, but he respected me enough not to force me to talk about anything I wasn't ready to. I'm not sure what you're trying to imply."

"I'm not trying to imply anything, dear. All couples have room to grow. I'm just pointing out something that I noticed, is all."

Sarah was upset, but had no interest in continuing the conversation any further. Her mother had only been home for one night and she didn't want to start fighting already. Plus, she knew her mother and it wouldn't be an easy fight to win. Eve was just as stubborn as she was. Isaac had always been non-confrontational and took his wife's lead. The entire meal was served and eaten in silence except for the occasional sigh from Eve. She was just giving her daughter advice. She couldn't see what all the fuss was about. So what if she thought Sarah and Isaac could work on their ability to communicate? Everybody could! Eve wished Sarah wouldn't take things so personally all the time. Sarah wished her mother wouldn't make things so personal.

After the meal, Sarah begrudgingly thanked her mother for cooking. Eve nodded in response, clearly still hurt by her daughter's response. Sarah sighed. Her mother had done this ever since she was a child. Whenever they had a disagreement Eve would silently pout until Sarah felt guilty enough to apologize. Even though she knew better by now, Sarah still couldn't help apologizing in order to resolve the situation.

"Okay, Mama, I'm sorry I snapped at you. I know you were just trying to help."

Eve's downturned face broke into a smile.

"Of course I forgive you, dear. I didn't mean anything by it."

Mother and daughter hugged each other stiffly. Eve felt light as a feather after hearing her daughter's apology, but Sarah was still salty. She was angry with herself for letting her mother manipulate her that way, especially as an adult. She wanted to enjoy her mother's visit, but if she kept acting this way it was going to prove difficult. Sarah couldn't help but dwell on it for the rest of the day.

***

"Sweetheart, not so much paprika. You don't want that stew to taste like it was cooked over an open fire, do you?"

"Mother, please. I've made stew before. I think I can do it without your help."

"Of course you've made stew before, you just haven't made it my way."

"I *like* the stew the way I make it."

"That's because you haven't tasted mine yet."

"That's it. I can't keep going back and forth with you like this. Go ahead and make the stew however you want. I'm through bickering with you."

"I don't know what you're so upset about, dear. You want to eat a delicious meal don't you?"

Sarah begrudgingly passed the spoon to her mother.

"Keep stirring. Don't let it burn."

"This isn't my first time in the kitchen, Sarah."

"Clearly."

Eve picked up where her daughter left off without missing a beat. First, she added only a pinch of paprika, just a dash of Worcestershire sauce, and a squeeze of lemon juice. It was not her intention to upset Sarah, but she firmly believed that mother does know best. Too much paprika would have overwhelmed the other flavors of the stew. She couldn't understand why Sarah wouldn't want to cook the best possible meal, even if she was wrong about how to do so.

As she stirred the simmering pot, Eve could just make out the whisper of her daughter's voice coming from the other room. She couldn't quite make out what she was saying, but it was clear from her tone that she hadn't yet let go of the incident in the kitchen. Isaac must be getting an earful; Sarah had never been short winded. *She'll change her tune once she has a bite of this stew,* Eve thought optimistically. She tossed a couple of chopped up carrots and a sprinkle of salt over her bubbling creation. The smell was nothing short of delightful, but as it wafted through the house it only made Sarah bristle even more.

"Isaac, this is the second time today she's stepped in where she doesn't belong."

"The woman's just trying to feed us, Sarah."

"I'm not talking about the kitchen. She thinks she knows best about everything and feels entitled to tell me what to do no matter if I want to hear it or not. It's been two days and she's already driving me up a wall, Isaac. How do I tell her that I'm an adult and she has to treat me like one?"

"Just like that, I think. She's a stubborn woman, but you're her daughter. She respects you and she'll listen to you."

Sarah could hear her mother singing to herself in the kitchen. She groaned.

"It's like she doesn't even know I'm upset. Either that, or she doesn't care."

"That's not it. You know your mother. She knows there's a problem, she just likes to pretend there isn't one."

Sarah looked unconvinced.

"You're both going through a lot right now. You need each other more than you need to fight with each other. Go talk to her."

"Okay."

Sarah steeled herself and walked into the kitchen to confront her mother. Eve pretended not to notice and continued singing while she stirred the stew, back turned to her daughter.

"Mama, I've got a bone to pick with you."

"Oh, what's the matter, dear?" Eve replied without turning to face her.

I just feel like you don't see me as a grownup wife and mother and you insist on treating me like a child. I don't like it and I'm asking for your respect."

"Sarah, of course I know you're a wife and mother, a good one too. You've raised two beautiful children with Isaac and you should be proud of that. I know I am, but I still am *your* mother, you know. It wouldn't hurt you to listen to my advice every once in a while."

"I do listen to your advice. When I ask for it. You've only been here for two days and you've already stuck your nose in to where it doesn't belong."

"Now what on earth are you talking about?"

"Mama, please, don't pretend you don't know what I'm referring to."

Eve shrugged defiantly, which only frustrated Sarah more.

"This morning at breakfast! You seem to think you know more about mine and Isaac's relationship than we do. It's not your place to offer unwelcome input. We have a blessed and happy marriage, but I'm sorry if it doesn't conform to your ideas of what a marriage should look like. I'm sure you and Papa didn't have a spotless forty-eight years."

Sarah was right. After Eddie's passing, Eve had focused so much on the good memories she didn't have time to remember the bad. She had once had a miscarriage, right before she had Sarah, and she kept it from her husband. She was so ashamed and put all the blame of that failed pregnancy on her own shoulders. Was it something she did? Could she have prevented it? Instead of sharing these feelings with Eddie, she kept them bottled up. She stopped eating, couldn't sleep, and the effects were starting to show on her already petite frame. Eddie soon realized something was wrong and he pressed her on it until she came clean. When she finally told him, he held her tight and assured her that it wasn't her fault. Finally telling Eddie made her feel instantly relieved. At least half the burden of this tragic secret was now on someone else. She didn't have to go through it alone anymore.

Even if Sarah didn't want to hear it, that's why Eve knew she was right to speak up.

"You're right, Sarah. My marriage with your father wasn't perfect, but it was long. That's because we were constantly learning from our mistakes and growing together. I've already been through the things you and Isaac are dealing with now. As your mother, all I wanted to do was make things a little easier for you. Is that a sin?"

"I'm grateful to you for wanting what's best for me, I really am, but you have to let *me* decide what's best for me. I want to be able to figure these things out on my own. I don't need a cheat sheet."

"It's not a 'cheat sheet,' it's just a little guidance from someone who's already been there."

"Wait for me to ask for it then."

"You're just as pigheaded as I am, Sarah. You'd never ask for my help. Besides, I have to think of Aaron and Beth, too. What's going to happen to them if their parents are too wrapped up in their marriage to pay them any attention?"

"You're criticizing my ability to be a good mother now? Are you serious?"

"No, no, no, dear, you're a wonderful mother. I'm just telling you why it's so important that you listen to my advice."

"No. This is enough, mother. I know you and Papa used to live here and you still might feel some sort of claim to this house and the people inside of it, but no more of this. This is *my* house. This is *my* family. You haven't visited us here in seventeen years. You don't just get to waltz in now and act like you never left. I'm sorry, but I don't need your advice. If you want to stay here, in my house, you need to respect my wishes. I love you, Mama, but I can't live like this."

Sarah stormed off to her room to decompress, leaving Eve dumbfounded in the kitchen. Her daughter had never talked back to her like that before. Eve realized how much pain her daughter must be in after losing her father, but couldn't help but be hurt by Sarah's words. She heard Isaac rush to their bedroom to speak with his wife. Spoon still in hand, she could smell the stew burning behind her.

***

After such an explosive argument with her daughter, Eve was desperate to relax. It was too late to take a walk, but any amount of fresh air would help. She walked out to the porch and sat down in the rocking chair. The back-and-forth motion soothed her, but she was still fuming. She had just been trying to help make dinner for her family. Why did Sarah have to turn that into some sort of power play? Eve knew a better way to make the stew. Why should that hurt her feelings? *I raised that girl,* Eve thought, *you'd think she'd trust me by now.*

This is my house, mother. My family.

The words rang in Eve's ears like a siren. She was at the same time hurt by them and also knew why Sarah had said them. It was her choice, after all, to stay away for so long. What did she expect? Eve was beginning to soften. She knew the hurt she had caused wouldn't be easy to forgive, but she still felt entitled to some respect. This was her house first. She created this family, with Eddie's help of course, but Eddie wasn't here now. It was her responsibility to lead this family now, even if she had neglected that role in the past, even if Sarah didn't always want her advice. *Mother knows best,* she thought as she accidentally drifted off to sleep on the porch.

A couple hours later, Eve was awoken by a set of creaky footsteps walking past her. She opened her eyes to see Beth, dressed in day clothes and covered by a hood, sneaking down the front steps. She must have been too nervously focused on sneaking out to notice her grandmother sleeping soundly in the rocking chair. When Eve realized what was going on, she didn't make any moves to stop her granddaughter, but she was curious. Beth wasn't the type to get into any real trouble, but aside from that there was no way to know what exactly she was up to. If she had any reason to be concerned she'd have followed Beth, or stopped her outright, but she didn't. Why ruin the girl's night and get her into trouble for no reason? Eve decided to pull her granddaughter aside the next day to ask about her midnight rendezvous, but for now she went to her room to finish her night's sleep. A rocking chair on a farmhouse porch was no place for a woman her age to spend the night.

In the morning, Eve found herself on the porch once again, this time at an appropriate hour with a cup of coffee in her hands. Also once again, Beth almost didn't see her grandmother sitting there as she walked out the door on her way to town. Eve pointedly cleared her throat to get the young girl's attention. Beth jumped, startled to learn that there was someone on the porch with her.

"Good morning, sweetheart. Sleep well last night?"

Beth nodded and took a step forward in an attempt to leave.

"Not so fast, dear. Don't you want to sit on the porch with me and enjoy this lovely morning? This is one of my favorite spots to sit and watch the world go by. It's amazing how much you can learn about a person just by watching them go about their day...or night."

Beth's face flushed and her eyes went wide. The normally quiet girl then let loose a waterfall of information.

"Nana, please don't tell Ma or Pa or Aaron. I promise I wasn't getting into any trouble. Collin just has so much to do during the day. His father never lets him have any free time during farming season. All we do is talk, I swear. He's a really great guy, Nan, but Ma and Pa would never let me leave the house by myself at night, especially not to see a boy. We don't even go into his house. We just sit on his porch and one time he held my hand but he's never tried anything. He wants to take over the family farm one day, that's why he does whatever his father says or else we'd be able to meet during the day."

Eve threw her head back and laughed.

"Oh my! I don't think you've said that many words since the day you were born. I'm not going to tell your parents, or your brother. I trust your judgment, dear. You've got a strong head on your shoulders."

Beth relaxed a little, but not entirely. She squared her shoulders and looked defiantly at her grandmother.

"Please don't ask me to stop seeing him, Nan, because I won't. I love him. We're going to get married and I'm going to live with him on his families farm."

"Darling girl, I wouldn't dream of standing in the way of true love, but if you really do feel this way please let me meet this boy. You're a smart girl, but I have many decades of experience on you."

"I don't know. It would be difficult to find a free moment for us all to talk without drawing suspicion."

"The boy goes to church, doesn't he?"

Beth hesitantly nodded.

"I'll talk to this dashing young man after the service tomorrow, then. You can't deny an old lady a word at church."

"I guess that would be okay. Just don't let our parents hear. If they knew what we've been up to we'd never see each other again."

"You're secret's safe with me. Go on now, and when you're in town pick your grandmother up some herbal tea, will you? Tea helps your old Nana sleep soundly through the night," Eve said with a wink.

"I will, Nan. Thank you."

Beth leaned down to give Eve a quick peck on the cheek and sprinted of towards town.

New love, Eve mused. She wondered if she'd ever be disillusioned to it. After all these decades, she thought not. She and Eddie did their fair share of sneaking around when they still lived with their parents. After the Sunday sing it was expected that the young couples would drive home together in their buggies and spend some time chatting in their families' homes while their parents slept, but the remaining six nights of the week were different. If she and Eddie wanted to see each outside of a formal function they'd have to do so without their parents permission. She remembered the small pond, set back from the road, almost exactly halfway between their homes where they'd sometimes meet.

There was one particularly moonlit night when Eve broke through the tree line surrounding the pond to find a candlelit picnic waiting for her. On the blanket, Eddie laid out a spread of bread and cheeses, a small pie, and a bottle of wine he had stolen from his lush of an uncle who kept a stash under the floorboards of his house. They sat together under the stars sipping wine, feeding each other bites of cheese, and talking about their future together. This was the first time Eddie told her he was going to marry her one day.

He said, "Eve, you're it. I'd follow you anywhere, even the moon," and he pointed to the sky.

Eve laughed and pointed to the pond.

"How about there?"

It took no time at all for Eddie to strip down to his undergarments and dive into the water. When he emerged, smiling, he yelled to her.

"It's freezing, Eve! I trusted you. Get in here and warm me up."

No one but her own mother had ever seen her in anything less than a nightgown before. She felt shy about taking off her clothes, but that feeling was overwhelmed by excitement. She wanted Eddie to see her soft, pale skin in the moonlight. She had not been rail-thin as a teenager, but her womanly curves were pleasant and she carried them with grace. She didn't want Eddie to know, but she made a show of taking of her clothing. Piece by piece, she removed everything but her bra and panties until she was glowing on the bank in front of him.

"I've never seen anything like you," he said before being hit by a wall of water from Eve's cannonball.

Her head hadn't even broken the surface before he swept her up into his arms. With no one around to see, he held her close and kissed her on the mouth, then her cheek, her ear, her neck, and her shoulder. She had goose pimples from the chill of the water, but not only that. She couldn't help but want to see what else he would kiss, but stripping down to her underwear and drinking wine with a boy in the middle of the night was as far as she was willing to go. When his hands started to slide further down her back she playfully splashed him and swam away. He would never push her, but he was definitely placed less value on his own virtue, at that time at least. This wouldn't be the last time they met up at that pond, but it would be the last time she swam away.

Eve was a little concerned about if Beth and Collin had an equivalent of "meeting at the pond" but she couldn't worry herself too much about it. She refused to be one of those hypocritical old ladies. Do as I say, not as I do. Besides, Beth was smart. It was more this boy that she was concerned about. She'd feel better once she met him. Even though she trusted Beth's opinion of him, she knew what teenaged boys were like. She'd feel better once she spoke to him. Even the nicest boys could benefit from a few words of wisdom on how to properly treat a woman.

***

That week, it was the Gingriches' turn to hold church service. Twenty or so families from town gathered in their quaint living room for the morning sermon. Young children sat with their parents, while the older kids and teens sat separately, sorted by gender. From the back of the room, Eve watched Beth exchange flirtatious glances with a boy who had a curly mop of hair and wide smile across the room who must have been Collin. She could see herself and Eddie in the pair and it made her happy and sad at the same time. She wanted to protect the pureness of it all. Hopefully, there love will only get stronger, but it will never be as new as it is now. The deacon began the sermon and the two teenagers snapped to attention, but Eve was still list in thought.

After the final prayer, Eve waited in her seat until the children started filing out of the room. Just as Collin was about to pass her, she began making a big show of trying to get out of her seat. Exaggeratedly mumbling and groaning to herself, Collin moved to help her. *Good boy,* she thought.

"Excuse me, ma'am. Please let me help you out of your seat."

"Why, thank you, young man. These old bones aren't what they used to be."

Collin lightly grabbed her by the crook of her arm and escorted her to the door. Eve could see Beth watching nervously from the lawn.

"There you are, ma'am."

Collin dipped his chin as a goodbye, but Eve was not quite finished with him yet.

"Ohhh," she groaned, placing her hands on her lower back, "it's such a long walk back home."

"Would you like me to walk you home, ma'am?"

Eve smiled, "That would be lovely, dear."

Beth watched her grandmother and her boyfriend walk off together, but was helpless to follow. Sarah and Isaac had her trapped in a conversation with the Gingriches about what book she was currently reading. Eve made sure she and Collin had gotten out of earshot before she began her questioning.

"It's Collin, isn't it?"

"Yes, ma'am."

"Oh, 'ma'am' makes me feel old. Besides, you're practically family now, going steady with my granddaughter. Please, call me Eve."

The good-natured farm boy froze and his face paled. Beth had apparently not warned him that she wanted to talk to him.

"Dear, don't worry, I'm not going to get you in trouble. I'm not going to tell either of your parents. I just wanted to have a little chat with the boy my granddaughter sneaks out to see at night."

Collin continued walking, but was still wary.

"I'd like to get to know you a little better, is all."

"Okay," Collin responded, unconvinced.

"How old are you, son?"

"Sixteen."

"Ah, Beth's got her eye on an older man. Makes sense. She's an old soul and too smart for her own good."

"Beth's very smart. She always lends me books to read and always tells me details about it that I never even noticed while I was reading. No one has a mind like hers."

"I'm glad that you can appreciate how special she is, but don't let her intelligence fool you. She's still a fourteen-year-old girl and has the maturity of one. You have to be sensitive of that."

"Mrs. Miller, with all due respect, I don't know if you're giving Beth enough credit. She's the most mature person I know, more mature than my parents sometimes. Don't get me wrong, I treat her right, but it she'd be furious with me if I treated her like a child."

"Collin, sometimes Nana knows best. Trust me, young love can blind a girl to the things that matter."

Eve was speaking from experience. She didn't regret her relationship with Eddie for an instant, but there were some things she could have done better. There were days when she skipped out on her chores or her studies so she could meet Eddie by the pond. Once, she was so distracted by the prospect of seeing him that she left the gate to the pigpen open after she finished feeding them. She came back home a few hours later to her parents and siblings running all over the neighborhood trying to chase down the escaped animals. Eve was not allowed to leave the house except for church for a whole month after that.

"I'm not distracting Beth, believe me. I won't see her for days at a time because she's too busy finishing a book she's wrapped up in."

"That's good. I've seen plenty of young girls throw away their hobbies for the sake of new lover."

Collin blushed at Eve's use of the word "lover."

"Son, it may be hard to believe but I was a teenager myself once. I know how these things go. I knew when to say "no," but most girls might not. It's up to the young man to draw the boundaries. Never pressure a woman to do anything she doesn't want to do."

"I would never...I mean, I wouldn't dream about...I couldn't..."

"Collin, Collin, I'm not accusing you of anything. You seem like a nice boy. I don't think you would do anything like that to Beth. I just wouldn't be doing my job as a grandmother if I didn't give you a few words of advice."

Advice? thought Collin, *more like words of warning.*

Eve didn't realize that the words she thought of as helpful were coming off as more of a threat. She had good intentions for her granddaughter and her new beau, but the execution left much to be desired. They spent the remainder of the walk to Eve's home silent. She thought they were just enjoying each other's company, but Collin was terrified about what else might come out of Eve's mouth. When they finally made it to her porch, he could barely look her in the eyes.

"Thank you for the delightful walk home, young man. I'm glad we got the chance to get to know each other. I look forward to seeing you again soon."

"My pleasure," Collin mumbled before quickly nodding his head goodbye and turning on his heel. He didn't slow his pace down to less than a brisk walk all the way home.

***

It was almost suppertime when Beth returned home, tears in her eyes. Eve was in the kitchen prepping vegetable for the meal when she heard the small, but angry footsteps march up behind her. She turned around to see quiet little Beth fuming with rage.

"How could you, Nan? You said you just wanted to get to know him, not interrogate him!"

"Beth, I did want to get to know him and his character. What are you getting so upset about? We had a lovely chat."

"You scared him half to death, Nan! He told me he didn't know if he wanted to see me anymore because of what you said to him."

Beth broke down in tears.

"Oh, dear, come here," Eve reached out to embrace her granddaughter but Beth shirked away, "I truly don't know what all the fuss is about."

"You...you told him I wasn't...*mature* enough for a relationship. You told him to...be careful with me." She said through the sniffles. "Now he's afraid to even hold my hand in case he upsets me and I tell my parents or you. Why did you have to do that?"

"Beth, please, I was only looking out for your best interests. You're a fourteen-year-old girl, of course you're not as mature as a grown woman! Even the nicest boys should be reminded, from time to time, to treat their girlfriend right. There's no harm in that."

"You're wrong! Collin was treating me just fine before you stepped in. I'm mature enough to handle my own relationship, Nan. If I knew you were going to threaten him I never would have agreed to let you talk to him. I trusted you and you ruined my relationship."

"If this boy has been scared off so easily by a few words from an old woman, maybe you're better off without him anyways."

"I love him, and he loves me. This would have never happened if you just stayed at home. I wish you never came here!"

At that, Beth ran off to her room and slammed the door shut. *Why do these things keep happening to me?* Eve thought. *And always in the kitchen, too.* She tried not to take it to heart. Beth was a teenage girl and teenage girls were overly emotional. She probably took something Collin said out of context and overreacted. She'd get over it eventually and those two kids will go on sneaking out in the middle of the night to meet each other as usual. Eve didn't regret anything she had said to Collin. She wanted the best for her granddaughter and she was willing to take a few punches to ensure it. Eve went back to chopping the vegetables and began to hum in order to drown out the muffled cries coming from Beth's room. This was another thing she knew about teenagers; sometimes you just had to let them cry it out.

Beth didn't come out of her room for supper. Sarah threatened to break the door down while Isaac tried to persuade her to open it, but neither tactic worked. Sarah was so emotionally exhausted because of the last couple of days she finally just gave up. The remaining Millers sat around the table in uncomfortable silence, which was sometimes broken up by Isaac or Aaron's unsuccessful attempts at light conversation, until the end of the meal. The moment Sarah finished eating she got up from the table without a word and went to her room. Isaac mumbled a polite "Thank you for cooking, Eve" and followed in his wife's footsteps. Eve sighed sadly into her plate. She knew this was all happening because of her, but she couldn't understand why her attempts at helping had been taken so poorly. Aaron noticed how sad his grandmother looked and attempted to consol her.

"Nana, don't look so glum. I'm so happy that you're here."

"Thank you, dear, but you don't have to try to cheer me up. Everyone's been sour since the moment I got here. Beth was right. Maybe I should have stayed home."

"Don't say that! Beth's always been sour and Ma and Pa have troubles of their own, even if they never want to admit it. They're all just looking for someone to blame their problems on."

Eve smiled gratefully at her grandson. It was kind of him to try and comfort her, but she knew it wasn't true. She was always sticking her nose in where it didn't belong; she just didn't think her own family was one of those places. It served her right, she guessed, for being absent for so long. They learned to get along without her. On the one hand, she should have been proud of their self-sufficiency, but on the other, she missed being needed.

"I may have overstayed my welcome. It seems you've outgrown your old Nana."

"Don't be silly, Nan. We could never outgrow you. Just let everyone sleep on it and I'm sure they'll all feel better in the morning. I'm going to go to sleep, too, actually. I have to get to my apprenticeship bright and early tomorrow morning. I'm working on something special for you. Goodnight, Nan."

Aaron leaned down to kiss Eve on the cheek and want off to his room. The boy was always thinking about other people. She was touched by his intention to make her a gift, but couldn't help but feel like she didn't deserve it. Maybe Aaron was right and they all could use a good night's sleep. Eve cleaned up the table, washed the dishes, and went to sleep. Hopefully she'd be able to shake this feeling and be back to her old self by morning.

Unfortunately, things did not resolve themselves overnight. Eve felt a little bit better come sunrise, but was still worried about how her family was feeling as she sipped a cup of tea on the porch. Aaron had already passed her by and given her a hug on his way out the door. Now, she was anxiously waiting for her remaining family members to wake up. Beth was the first to leave her room. Eve could hear her shuffling around the kitchen looking for breakfast. Eve didn't feel like making a meal that morning. Isaac and Sarah soon followed, and the three of them had a quiet conversation in the kitchen.

"Ma, Pa, I've got to tell you both something and I don't want you to get upset, okay?"

"Well that's not exactly a good start, is it?" Sarah replied suspiciously.

"Just trust me, please."

Isaac squeezed his wife's hand and nodded at her, compelling Sarah to listen.

"Okay, sweetheart. What is it?"

"I've been going steady with a boy from town for quite a while now..."

"A boy! What boy? How long have you been seeing him? Why haven't you told us?"

"Ma, please! Let me finish. His name is Collin and he's working to take over his family's farm and we're in love.

Sarah began to interrupt again but Beth kept talking.

"I'm only telling you this because Nana found out and ruined everything! She talked to Collin after church yesterday and scared him off. Now he doesn't want to see me anymore and it's all her fault. I don't want Nana around anymore. If she goes home Collin might not be afraid to be with me anymore."

"What do you mean, 'Nana scared him off?' What did she say?"

"She told him I wasn't mature enough for a relationship and to be careful with me. Now he's afraid I really am too immature and won't offer me rides in his buggy anymore just in case Nana sees and thinks he might be getting fresh with me."

"Well, does he get fresh with you?"

"Pa, no! I don't want to talk about this stuff. I just want you to tell Nana that she has to go home."

"Honey, I'm sorry Nana got between you and this boy, but she's family. We can't just kick her out when she's got no one to go to back home. Things have been tough for all of us since Grandpa Eddie passed, but just try to imagine what it must be like for her. I wouldn't feel right about sending her home to stay in that house all by herself."

Isaac attempted to come to Eve's defense, but Sarah was still just as upset at her mother as she was the day before. And now, hearing her daughter's pleas, she was almost convinced sending Eve home would be the right thing to do.

"Isaac, Beth might have a point. She's only been here a couple of days and she's driving me crazy. I thought she might be lonely back at home and wasn't reaching out because of her stubbornness, but now I think she was just as content to be alone. I tried talking to her like you said, but it only made things worse. I think it's time for my mother to go home."

Isaac was not totally happy with that decision, but supported his wife's choice.

"If you think that's what's best then we should ask her to leave, but I'm still a little hesitant about it. Aaron's been very happy to have her here. I know he'd been waiting for her to come visit for some time now. It might upset him to send her home so soon."

"Aaron can drive her home then and spend some quality time with her on the road. He can borrow the Gingriches' car, I'm sure they won't mind."

"Alright, dear. That seems like as fair a compromise as we'll be able to make, but you should be the one to tell her."

Sarah agreed, but the sound from their conversation had drifted out onto the porch and Eve had heard the whole thing. She was devastated. She knew things were getting tense between them, but she had no idea that her presence made them feel this badly. She felt a little bit guilty, but mostly hurt. If her own family didn't want her around, who would?

Sarah walked out onto the porch to confront her mother for the second time. Her face was grim, but not as grim as her mother's.

"Mama, I've got to talk to you."

"No need. I heard the whole conversation. I don't need to relive that pain again."

"I'm sorry you had to hear it that way, but I think it's for the best. You've caused a lot of stress for us since you've been here and you were perfectly content at home all this time since Papa dies until I invited you to come out to stay with us."

Sarah paused to give her mother a chance to speak, but Eve remained silent.

"Aaron will drive you home. That way you'll get to spend some more time with him on the way."

"Yes, I heard the first time. That will be fine."

Eve couldn't look at her daughter. She felt so betrayed. She couldn't bring herself to say anything else. She could only purse her lips and look out at the street in front of her. Sarah stood by for a moment before she realized she wouldn't be able to get another word out of her mother.

"I wish it didn't have to be this way," she said as she turned her back to Eve and went back into the house. Sarah paused in the doorway. "You'll want to start packing soon. Aaron will be finished with his apprenticeship by noon."

Eve got up out of her chair and walked off the porch without a word. That was the final straw. Did Sarah stop to tell her to pack up just to hurt her? Was she really that callous? Eve needed to talk a walk to calm down. She couldn't face her family just yet. She didn't have a destination in mind, she just kept walking until eventually she realized she had made her way to her and Eddie's old pond.

The clearing seemed smaller than she remembered, but the water was just as clear. She peered over the edge, hoping to see the young woman she once was in her reflection, but she only saw the woman she was now. Skin wrinkled with age, not laughter, eyes red and swollen, she had cried the whole walk to the pond. She let her hair down with one, boney hand. The salt and pepper strands fell around her shoulders and in front of her face, obscuring her reflection. A few shimmering pieces fell into the water. Eve hadn't worn her hair down since she was just a girl, but now it only made her look strange, like an old woman pretending to be young.

"I'm not pretending to be anything," she whispered to her reflection, "I'm just figuring out how to be me."

In that moment, Eve realized it wasn't Eddie that she had been missing it had been herself. For forty-eight years she had been married. For forty-eight years every decision she made, everything she did, every thought in her head included him in some way. She couldn't remember what life was like before him. That didn't mean she hadn't been missing him, mourning him, and loving him, but she had made peace with the fact that he was gone long ago. Now, she mourned her identity as part of a couple. The life she had grown used to living was gone and she had no idea how to live as an independent woman. She thought she would find happiness with her family, and she was not entirely wrong, but she couldn't rely entirely on them. It was just replacing one relationship with another when what she really needed was to learn how to be alone.

Eve laughed out loud in the middle of the woods. It seemed so simple now. She had always defined herself by the people around her and now that she was all alone by the pond she felt more like herself than she ever had. She began to strip of her clothes, piece by piece, until she was completely nude on the bank. Her hair softly whipped around her face and she felt the warm breeze on her exposed skin. Taking off her clothes for Eddie that night was something special, but this, standing naked for no one but herself, was something completely new.

A smile spread across Eve's face as wide as she could manage and she dove into the glimmering pool. The icy water chilled her whole body. She stayed submerged for as long as she could before needing to take a breath. In the silence under the surface she felt truly alone, and for the first time it felt freeing rather than stifling. *Goodbye, Eddie. I hope to see you again one day, but until I do I'm going to enjoy my time here. I hope that isn't a problem, my love.* Eddie couldn't answer her, but she felt as though he was smiling down at her from just above the surface, but when she broke through and gulped in a lungful of air no one was there. ***

Aaron was waiting for her on the porch when Eve finally returned to he house. His solemn expression was interrupted by one of confusion when he realized his grandmother was soaking wet.

"Nana, what happened to you?"

"Your old Nan just went for a quick swim is all. Nothing to worry about."

Eve squeezed some of the leftover water out of her hair onto the ground with a smile. She thought she might leave it down for a little while.

"Are you alright?"

"More than, dear. Would you mind waiting a moment while I pack up my things? I seem to have gotten a little of course, or back on maybe."

"Sure, Nan. Just let me know when you're ready and I'll help you with your bags," Aaron agreed, confused but not willing to push his grandmother for more information.

Eve tracked wet footprints through the halls as she made her way to her former bedroom. The rest of the family was nowhere to be seen. No doubt keeping themselves busy to keep from having to face the woman they'd just asked to leave. This didn't bother Eve as much as she thought it might. A little distance might do them good. They'll cool of and next time they see each other Eve won't put so much pressure on them to make her happy. She was in charge of that now.

Her diary sat on the nightstand, one empty page left in the back. She didn't want to fill it quite yet, but she knew what she would write when she did. The cover felt smooth as silk as she ran her fingers over it before packing it away with the rest of her things. Her suitcase quickly filled with items of clothing. Eve realized she had never gotten around to passing out the collection of knitted hats and scarves to her family members. She'd leave the bag with Aaron. The final thing to be packed up was the scarf she had thrown over the mirror on her first night back. That was only a couple days ago but it might as well have been years. She felt like a completely different person than she was when she arrived.

Eve pulled the scarf from the mirror and look at herself. Her was beginning to dry in soft waves that framed her face. She was smiling and the wrinkles around her eyes and mouth looked purposeful. She felt as though she'd earned them instead of been burdened by them. She didn't look youthful, she never would again, but she looked happy. Eve picked up her belongings and met Aaron outside.

"Nan, I told you I'd help you with those. You shouldn't be carrying so much weight."

"It's nothing at all, dear. I promise."

Still, he swooped in to grab the bags and put them in the trunk. Aaron opened the passenger side door and helped Eve inside. From her seat she could see her family peering out from one of the windows. They looked at her with pity mixed with sadness and guilt.

"Please, tell your Ma and Pa and Beth not to feel bad. It really is better this way. When you get back, tell them that Nana loves them dearly and she'll see them again soon."

"Okay, Nan. I will, but I do have to say I'm surprised at how you're handling this. They weren't very fair to you."

"I was not very fair to them either. I expected too much of them and it was selfish. Don't you worry, though, I know everything will turn out alright."

"If you say so, Nan."

Aaron started the car and pulled away from the house. Eve didn't wave at her family, but she didn't take her eyes off of them until she was too far away to make out their silhouettes in the window. The pair drove on for sometime in silence before Eve suddenly spoke up.

"Dear, if you don't mind, can we stop by Grandpa Eddie's grave? I've got something I need to say to him."

"Sure, Nan. I can do that for you."

Aaron turned off the main road and followed a familiar winding path through the woods. This was not the first time Aaron had visited his grandfather. The first few weeks after his death, Aaron would sneak out of the house in the middle of the night and walk all the way to the graveyard. Sometimes he'd bring flowers, or even a piece of cheese or some other snack that he knew Grandpa Eddie would like. He'd sit with his back up against the headstone and tell his grandfather everything: what he learned at his apprenticeship, small fights that head get into with Beth, and sometimes just what he had for lunch that day. Despite his good faith in people, Aaron often thought it was easier to talk to the dead than the living, which is why he completely understood his grandmother's need to make the trip out to see Grandpa Eddie's grave.

Eventually, they came upon a large clearing smattered with headstones. The gate was too small to let a car through so Aaron parked right outside.

"Would it be okay if I went on my own first? I just need a few moments alone with him."

Aaron nodded and stayed in his seat as he watched his grandmother walk towards the grave marked "Edward Miller." When she got close enough to read the name she fell to her knees. Tears fell from her eyes, but the smile never left her face.

"My dearest love, my Eddie. I'm so happy to talk to you. I've got some good news and some bad news for you, dear. I no longer miss you, but please don't be upset. The good news is I'll never stop loving you, not for one single moment. I've just realized some things over the past couple of days. I finally went back home to visit our amazing daughter and her family. I thought it would be difficult to go back to that house where we started our life together, and I wasn't wrong, but it wasn't nearly as painful as I anticipated. I felt closer to you than I had in a long time. It was a comfort, but one I couldn't rely on, unfortunately. Even though you felt closer, Eddie, you weren't and that's what I realized. I can't rely on you anymore, not entirely. I have to be my own person for the first time in my life. I'm terrified, but so much lighter. And even though you're gone, it's because of you, because of the life you and I had together, that I know I'm going to make it alone."

Eve lay down on top of the grave and let herself sob. She let the tears flow freely from her eyes and water the grass underneath her. She imagined the water made it all the way to Eddie's flower-printed socks and gave the blooms new life. Her body shook and wailed, but it wasn't tragic and it wasn't painful, it was release. Every tear felt like a small weight falling out of her, making her lighter and lighter until she was floating on air. She rose up out of her body and looked down on herself, now lying on her back. The floating Eve thought the crying Eve looked peaceful, her eyes looking up at the sky and one hand over her heart. She reached down to stroke her own cheek when Aaron rushed over yelling "Nana!" over and over again. Eve's out of body experience was cut short. She was having a heart attack.

***

Eve woke up a day later in an unfamiliar bed with Aaron sitting next to her. He was reading a book, eyes glimmering emotionally. It took a moment for Eve to realize that she was in a hospital bed. Wires and tubes connected to her body like roots. The plain white hospital gown felt like paper against her skin. She turned her head to look at Aaron and noticed that the book he was reading was her diary.

"You're a nosy boy, aren't you?"

Aaron jumped in his seat, startled by his grandmother's sudden consciousness.

"Nan! You're awake! I'm sorry I was reading your diary. I...I didn't know if you were going to wake up and I thought...you might have written about what you might want to happen to you if that were to...happen."

"That's very thoughtful, dear, but you don't have to put me in a box quite yet."

Aaron laughed uncomfortably at his grandmother's joke. She still didn't seem to realize how close she'd come to actually staying in that graveyard for good.

"Nana, you had a heart attack. The paramedics had to revive you on the scene. You...you died three times in the ambulance. The doctors only stabilized you late last night. No one knew if you were going to wake up."

The reality of the situation hit Eve all at once. She had come so close to death, just as she had finally started to live. She didn't have a bucket list or dream that needed to be realized, she just simply wanted to enjoy a few more years of happiness before she was reunited with Eddie. Eve wanted to be able to tell him what a good life she had, not how terrible the last stretch of it was after he left. She wanted him to be proud of her. It wasn't her time to go just yet.

"I'm sorry I gave you a scare. My heart isn't as strong as it used to be but it's still hanging on. I won't be going anywhere anytime soon."

"Nana, I wish it was as simple as that. The heart attack wasn't just a one-time thing. The doctors say it's a symptom of something bigger. You're ill, Nan, and they don't think you're going to get better."

"What do you mean?"

"The doctors say you have five, maybe six months left."

Aaron began to cry at his grandmother's bedside. She grabbed his rough hand and squeezed.

"My darling grandson, please, don't be upset. No one looks forward to the end, but I'm excited about all things I'll be able to do before then. I finally felt truly happy for the first time since Grandpa Eddie died and I'm not about to let this spoil that happiness. Save your tears for later, hm? Your old Nan still has some life in her yet."

The sensitive young man didn't stop his tears right away, but he squeezed his grandmother's hand back and nodded.

"I love you, Nan."

"Oh, I love you, too, sweetheart. Very much."

As they sat together silently, Eve noticed that the rest of her family didn't seem to be around and felt relieved. They didn't need to be burdened with this weight right away. It would only add to their guilt and that was the last thing she wanted.

"You haven't told your mother about this, have you?"

"I was waiting for you to wake up before I called her."

"Please, don't. I don't want to worry everyone unnecessarily."

"Unnecessarily? Nan, this is serious. You're sick."

"Aaron, please. I'll tell them in due time, I will."

Aaron looked at her with suspicion.

"I promise, dear. Please. Keep my secret?"

He sighed, "Okay, but under one condition. You come back home with me and stay with us for a little while like you planned."

"Oh, Aaron, your mother made it clear that I wasn't welcome there. I don't think it would be such a good idea."

"Nana, I'm not letting you go home to an empty house. You need to be with family."

Eve could tell how strongly her grandson felt about this. Maybe things would be different after her revelation by the pond. At least, she would be different.

"What would we tell them? They can't know I'm ill. How would we explain you bringing me back?"

"We'll just say you're very sorry. You wanted to come back and apologize for the trouble you've caused but you really want to be around family. I'll insist you stay. I want to have you around, Nan. That's no lie."

"If you insist, I'll go back, but if they put up a fuss you'll turn right back around and drive me straight home, okay?"

"Okay, Nan."

"Promise me."

"I promise."

After a moment, Aaron put one hand over the cover of Eve's diary and turned to her.

"I didn't realize how difficult yours and Grandpa Eddie's marriage could be. I only saw the good things. I didn't know how much you two went through together, and how much you overcame. I'm sorry I read your diary, but I think I learned a lot just from the few pages I read. You're a strong woman, Nana. I'm lucky to have you in my life."

Eve was touched by her grandson's kind words. All she ever wanted was for her life to mean something, to pass on wisdom to her family. What was the point of learning from her mistakes if she couldn't help the people who came after her? The last page in her diary was still blank. She had one more chance to write something that mattered, something that she could pass on. Her diary wouldn't just be a collection of anecdotes to be buried with her. She wanted to make it into something that her family could look at after she was gone. It wouldn't be a manual for a happy life, she was no expert, but maybe a sort of guidebook, a collection of suggestions.

"Dear, you don't know how happy that makes me to hear. The best thing a grandmother can do is influence her grandchildren's lives for the better. Looks like I've got a little work to do with Beth before I go. It looks like you might be right. Coming back home with you is the best thing I can do right now."

"Thanks, Nan. You won't regret it. They need you as much as you need them, even if neither of you will admit it."

"I trust you, dear. Now, let's get me out of this hospital. These places always feel too sterile to me. Take me back to a place with a little grit. I'm ill, but I'm still a down-home Amish woman at heart."

***

Nerves began to creep up on Eve on their drive back to the farm. Her newly discovered illness was one thing, facing her family after their last interaction was another. She thought she'd have a little more time to prepare herself, build confidence, and learn to bite her tongue before she saw them again. Aaron was certain they'd welcome her back with open arms, even without knowing about the illness. He had always been optimistic. Eve tried to absorb some of his positivity, but the knot in her stomach persisted. She thought back on the last time she drove into town and how familiar things looked to her, but now it was all brand new territory.

When they pulled up to the house Eve could see Isaac sitting on the porch. It was near suppertime, so Sarah would be in the kitchen cooking. Isaac spotted Eve in the front seat of the car and immediately stood up to go inside. Eve took a deep breath as she watched Sarah rush out the front door, apron still on, with Isaac trailing not far behind her. She looked furious and surprised. Aaron stepped out of the car to confront his mother before she could begin her tirade.

"Ma, hold on now, don't be angry with Nan. I made her come back."

"Why, Aaron? We all agreed it would be better if she went back home."

"No, 'we all' did not agree. You all made that decision without even talking to me first. It wasn't fair. I like having Nan here and I want her to stay. Besides, she's very sorry for upsetting you and Beth. She wanted to come back and apologize. Is that alright?"

Sarah was still visibly angry, but stopped trying to push past Aaron to get to the car.

"I don't know Aaron. I don't want to feel on edge in my own home."

"Nan knows what she did wrong. She's not going to stick her nose anywhere it doesn't belong again. I promise. She promises."

Eve had been sitting quietly in the car while they had this conversation, but now she stepped out to face her daughter.

"Sarah, dear, I'm sorry about what happened before. I didn't mean to upset you. I was only trying to help, but I can see now I was only being meddlesome, not helpful. Please let me stay. I'd like to spend some time with my grandchildren, and with you, without this cloud of resentment hanging over us. Can we start over, dear? Pretend I only just showed up on your porch?"

Sarah ran her hands through her hair. She felt like she had been backed into a corner with no good option. She loved her mother, but was wary about her sincerity.

"I'm going to be honest with you, Mama, I'm not sure. I think you need to talk to Beth first. If she says it's okay for you to stay with us, then you can stay. "

"Okay, dear. Where is Beth?"

"Reading in her room. Go ahead and talk to her."

Eve walked past her daughter and into the house. She found Beth sitting on her bed with a book in hand. When Beth saw her grandmother a frown spread across her face.

"I thought you were supposed to be back home already, Nan."

"I was, but I wanted to come back and apologize. I shouldn't have meddled in your and Collin's relationship. It was not my place. I thought I was being helpful by offering you two some advice from an old widow, but you didn't ask for it. You're plenty mature, dear, and probably even more mature than I am. Collin is a lovely boy and I hope you two can reconcile. Please tell him not to worry about me. I won't be meddling anymore. Do you forgive me?"

Beth sat on her bed with her arms crossed.

"I don't know, Nan. You really shook him up."

"I'd offer to talk to him again, but I don't know if it would help."

"No, I don't think it would."

An awkward silence fell over the two women. Beth was unconvinced, but Eve was not ready to give up quite yet.

"Dear, will you go on a walk with me? I want to show you something."

"I guess."

Beth and Eve walked silently through town and down a familiar forest path until they ended up at Eve and Eddie's pond. Beth seemed confused, but Eve had a plan.

"Do you know where we are, dear?"

"It's a pond, Nan. What's so special about a pond?"

"This is the pond where your Grandpa Eddie and I would meet up on our midnight rendezvous. Grandpa Eddie was my Collin. I know how special it is to find someone you truly love so early on in life. Can I tell you a story?"

Beth nodded.

"When Grandpa Eddie and I first started seeing each other we decided to keep our relationship a secret from our parents. We weren't doing anything wrong, we just wanted it to be something only for us, a love that wasn't influenced by anyone or anything else. We did this successfully for the first couple of months. He'd give me rides home in his buggy after the Sunday sing and we'd sit in my living room, your living room, talking all night while my parents were asleep. During the week, we'd plan to go into town at the same time, meeting up in the aisles of the corner store to do our shopping together. We thought we were being sly, but we didn't fool anyone that saw us together.

Eventually one of my neighbors noticed Eddie's frequent visits and told my parents about him. They weren't upset that I was seeing him, but they were very unhappy that I kept it a secret. They warned me that I needed to let them know when and where I would be meeting Eddie from then on, or else they'd make sure I'd stop seeing him completely. I was so frightened of upsetting my parents any further that I told Eddie I couldn't see him at all. He was understandably upset and confused about my sudden change of heart. I couldn't even tell him why I made that decision. I was too emotional.

A couple weeks went by where we'd only see each other in church and occasionally in town. He'd always try to catch my eye, but I was too embarrassed to look at him. I had begun to regret my decision. One night, I woke up to little pebbles bouncing off my window. When I pulled back the curtain to see who was there, I saw Eddie with his buggy all dressed up in ribbons. He had tied one of his hats and ties to his horse and was smiling like a fool. I was so happy to see him that I ran out onto the lawn in my nightgown. He swept me up in his arms and put me in his buggy. He drove me here, chatting my ear off the whole way about a special place, just for us. He never even asked for an explanation for why I tried to break it off with him in the first place. Somehow he just knew that I still loved him and that it was only my hesitation keeping us apart.

We sat under the stars all night by the water, catching up on all the little things we missed during our time apart. For the most part, I kept my parents informed about when I saw Eddie, but we still snuck out to the pond every once in a while. I was afraid of the consequences some, but I feared not having our secret moments even more.

If you don't mind me saying, I think all Collin needs is to know that you'll stick with him no matter what. That's what makes the risk worth it."

Beth had been sitting on the bank silently listening to her grandmother's story with her arms wrapped around her knees. She had been angry about Eve's interference before, but was surprised by how candid this new side of her was.

"Nan, I don't know what to say. I figured you and Grandpa Eddie had it easy. You guys were together for so long without any problems."

Eve chuckled.

"My dear, your grandfather and I had plenty of problems, one of which being we hid every negative thing away from everyone around us, and sometimes each other. No relationship is without its struggles, especially the long ones. Sometimes you have to work even harder for the good moments." She paused to take in the moment she was having with her granddaughter right then. It was one of her hardest won moments yet, but it was worth it just to sit in peaceful silence with Beth in a place she loved so much. "If you love Collin, don't let anything stand in your way, not even your nosy old Nan."

Beth laughed with her grandmother for the first time since she arrived.

"Thanks, Nan. I'm sorry I was so sour before and made you leave. I know you were just trying to help. I'd like it if you'd stay with us again, but only if you want to."

"Of course I do. Let's head back and talk to your mother. I think she's still a bit cross with me."

***

Back on the farm, Sarah paced anxiously back and forth across the porch. She wanted so much to just forgive her mother and go on living happily with her while she visited, but she still wasn't convinced that Eve wouldn't continue being overbearing. Isaac tried to calm her down, urging her to give her mother the benefit of the doubt, but she remained unsure. It was only when she saw Eve and Beth walking up the road chatting and laughing that she began to relax. Beth was everyone's harshest critic. If she had forgiven her grandmother, Sarah should at least give her a chance.

"Ma, please let Nana stay. I know things haven't been easy, but that's just sometimes the way things are. You work hard to be with the people you love."

Eve smiled at Beth's use of her own words. It felt good to be heard. She looked her daughter's pursed lips and crossed arms.

"Maybe we should have a meal first, hm? Let's get some food in our bellies before we make any decisions. How does that sound?"

Sarah reluctantly nodded and wordlessly waved her family into the kitchen for supper. The family sat awkwardly around the kitchen table while Sarah served them plates of roast chicken, boiled vegetables, and hunks of bread. Aaron and Beth attempted to start conversation but their mother refused to engage and Isaac was too busy watching her anxiously to take part. The children eventually gave up and ate their meals in silence. Eve didn't want to push her daughter and waited until she was comfortable enough to start a conversation. Eventually, once she and Isaac cleared the plates and the children begrudgingly went off to their rooms for the evening, Sarah let out a big sigh and sat across from her mother.

"I don't want to feel this way, you know."

"I know, dear. I didn't mean to make you feel this way."

"You just bring me unnecessary stress sometimes. You make me feel like I'm unable to make decisions on my own, or do things correctly, which I know isn't true. You were gone for so long, Mama, and now you come back and treat me like a child again and I don't appreciate it. I'm a wife and a mother and I've been taking care of them and myself for seventeen years now. I...I want to *want* your advice, not feel like you think I need it."

"Sarah, I'm so sorry I made you feel that way and not like the capable, amazing woman, mother, and wife that I know you are. That wasn't my intention at all. I thought it was my job as a mother to give you all the best of me, but I didn't realize that the way I was doing it was by forcing it on you. That's not the way a mother should share her wisdom. She should wait until it's asked for."

"I respect you so much, Mama. You raised me with kindness, love, and intelligence that I couldn't have gotten anywhere else. I'm the woman I am today because of you and Papa. All I ask is that you treat me like that woman, and not the child from the past."

"I promise, my dear. I'll keep my spoon out of your stew."

Mother and daughter stood up and embraced each other. Sarah squeezed her mother tight, feeling for the first time that she truly understood her. This is the feeling she hope for when she first invited her mother out to stay with them.

"Please, stay with us? I'm sorry things got so messy before, but you're welcome here, Mama."

"I'd like nothing more, sweetheart, especially now. It's been quite a long day and I'd love to get some rest."

"Of course. Go ahead and take the master bedroom again. You can unpack in the morning. I'll take care of the dishes."

They smiled and gave each other one last hug before Eve went off to bed. Sarah watched her mother shuffle slowly down the hall and walk into her room. She turned back to the sink and began washing that night's dishes. She felt so light after seeing Eve and Beth reconcile, and especially after their own conversation. For the longest time she didn't think her mother would ever be able to change, and she certainly didn't expect it, but here they were. She truly believed that her mother had actually seen and understood where she went wrong. Sarah wondered what was responsible for Eve's sudden change of heart. Aaron must have said something to her. He'd always been the most empathetic member of their family.

Just then Aaron walked out of his room and into the kitchen. He startled his mother enough for her to drop a plate into the sink, but the water stopped it from breaking.

"Oh my, Aaron you scared me!"

"Sorry, Ma, I was just a little thirsty. I wanted to grab a glass of water but I waited until I heard Nana go to bed. Thanks for letting her stay. I'm really happy to have her here and I know you all will be too."

"I hope so, dear. I really do. What did you say to her in the car, anyways? Before she left she wouldn't even look at me, let alone apologize."

"Well, when we got in the car she seemed resigned to the idea of leaving, serene almost. I asked her if she was okay, and she said she was. She said to tell you all that she loved you and she'd see you soon. She asked me to stop at Grandpa Eddie's grave because she had something to say to him. I don't know what that was because I stayed in the car until I saw her pass out..."

"She did what?"

"I mean...she passed out...flowers to the other graves?"

"Nana fainted in the graveyard? We've got to tae her to a doctor! Someone her age could have all sorts illnesses. She could have pneumonia or the flu. Why didn't you tell me about this right away?"

"Ma, please calm down. I already took Nan to the hospital. Well, an ambulance did. She had a heart attack and the doctors don't think it's going to be her last one. Nan's really sick."

Sarah braced herself on the edge of the sink, dropping a plate on the ground this time and shattering it. Isaac came running out of their room to find the source of the crash.

"Sarah, what's going on? I heard something smash," Isaac said before seeing his wife, pale faced and standing amongst the remnants of the plate. "What's going on? Are you alright?"

Sarah couldn't speak. She fell into her husband's arms and began to cry. Aaron stepped in to inform his father.

"Nan's sick, Pa. Real sick. She had a heart attack at Grandpa Eddie's grave. I had knock on a whole bunch of doors to find someone with a phone so I could call the paramedics. They said she died three times in the ambulance."

Sarah let out a soft sob into Isaac's shoulder.

"The doctors say she has six more months. It's an illness they can't cure. Just something that sometimes happens with old age, they said. That's why I had to bring her back. She almost didn't come. She was too worried about what you all thought about her. I told her not to be silly, she needed to be with family, but she refused unless I promised not to tell you that she was ill. Now I've gone and broke that promise. Please, don't tell her that you know. She might insist on going back home again and she needs to be here with us, with her family."

Sarah was silent, but Isaac nodded.

"Okay, son. We'll keep it to ourselves. I'm sure your mother agrees. You're right. Nana needs to be with the people she loves, and that's us. It would also probably be best if we don't tell your sister. She'd be able to keep a secret, but I don't want to burden her with this information before it's necessary for her to hear it."

"Good idea, Pa. Beth would probably lock herself in her room more than she already does. We'd never see her except at suppertime."

"Sarah, dear, I know this is hard, but you have to stay strong, okay? Your mama's lived a full and beautiful life. Now, we all knew this day would come, we just didn't know when. I think this may be a blessing.

Now we can make sure these last few months are something special for her. We just have to be quiet about it so she doesn't realize that we know. She's a proud woman, just like you."

Sarah lifted her head off her husband's shoulder and he wiped the tears from her eyes. She managed a weak smile and a nod.

"I'm so glad that she wasn't taken from us in that graveyard. We would have never had the chance to make up like we did. I don't know if I could live with myself if the last interaction I had with my own mother was me kicking her out of my house. It is a blessing, Isaac, and it's not one I'm going to squander."

Isaac kissed his wife on the forehead and pulled her tightly to him. They stood like that for a moment, calmly rocking in place, before Isaac shooed Aaron of to bed.

"I'm proud of you, son. You've handled this situation with more maturity than I think anyone else of us could muster. Now, head off to bed and get some sleep. This has been an exhausting couple of days for us all."

Aaron wrapped his arms around both of his parents and went to his room. Isaac and Sarah held each other in the kitchen for a while before going to bed themselves. Once there, Sarah couldn't bring herself to fall asleep. She was still reeling from how close she came to being parentless. She spent all this time trying to convince her mother that she was independent and capable, but now the thought of not having her around anymore frightened her. Sarah thought that it was Eve that needed her, but she was beginning to realize that it was the other way around.

***

In the morning, the entire family sat around the table together for breakfast. Sarah did her best to act normally, but she couldn't make eye contact with her mother for longer than a couple of seconds. Isaac's usually cheerful nature was marred by the weight of pretending not to know about Eve's health. Luckily, Aaron was skilled at remaining optimistic through times of struggle and led the conversation as naturally as his family members would allow. But it was not long before Sarah couldn't keep her feelings bottled up.

"Okay, okay. I know things are tense because of me right now. You can stay, Mama. Please, stay."

"I would love nothing more, dear. Thank you for giving me another chance."

Eve stood up from the table and began to walk across the kitchen to hug her daughter when she stopped suddenly. A confused look crossed over her face as she put one hand on the table to brace herself and the other clutched her chest. Another heart attack. Aaron recognized the symptoms immediately and rushed to his grandmother's aid just quickly enough to catch her as she fell to the floor.

The town physician arrived soon after. Beth had run into to town to find him. He pulled Sarah and Isaac aside to update them on Eve's condition. The second heart attack didn't cause her to faint this time, but it did leave her weaker than before. It wouldn't be necessary to take her to a hospital; there was nothing they'd be able to do for her there. The physician recommended putting her on bed rest and making her as comfortable as possible.

"It wouldn't be long," he said, "all you can do for her now is be there for her during her final moments."

Tears welled up in Sarah's eyes. Isaac took her hand.

"But the doctors at the hospital said she had months left to live, not days."

"That was before she had the second heart attack. It's weakened her considerably," he paused when he saw the fallen faces in front of him. "Look, sometimes doctors are wrong about these things. I might be wrong, but I think it's better to prepare for the worst instead of being surprised by it. There's always a chance she'll regain her strength and live happily for the next six months, but it's best to be realistic with these situations. She's an old woman, her heart is not as strong as it used to be. My advice would be to have someone stay with her through the night. Take shifts. I wouldn't leave her on her own, just in case."

"Thanks, doctor. We appreciate all your help."

Isaac shook the physician's hand.

"Of course. I'm just sorry I couldn't give you better news."

The physician touched Sarah lightly on the shoulder before he walked out. She tried to muster up a thank you but she could only manage to open her moth slightly. No words came out.

Propped up in the first bed she and her husband shared, Eve struggled to breathe normally. Every small action took a huge effort. Even so, a smile remained on her face in order to sooth the family members that surrounded her bed and refused to leave her side. Sarah's eyes were red-rimmed but it seemed she had finally run out of tears. Isaac stood behind his wife, squeezing her shoulders every once in a while to show his support. Beth sat next to her brother, who never took his eyes off of her, distractedly reading a book. She had reread the same page almost fifty times because she couldn't quite keep her mind off her ailing grandmother for long enough. Her parents thought it best not to tell her that they had known about Eve's illness before the second heart attack. It would only add to the confusion.

It was getting late and everyone in the room began to feel the pull of sleep, except for Eve. She was weak, but alert. Isaac noticed his children drifting off and Sarah's head leaning heavily on his arm.

"I'll stay up with Nana. You all should get some rest. I'll come wake one of you up when it's time to change shifts."

No one put up much of an argument and they all went off to bed after kissing Eve on the cheek and telling her they loved her. Isaac took a seat in the chair Sarah was sitting in and held Eve's hand.

"If you'd like to go to sleep, too, I'll be here. I don't mind."

"No thank you, dear. I don't feel tired in the slightest."

"Alright, Eve. I'll stay up with you."

"Do you know any good stories, Isaac? Would you humor a dying old lady with one?"

"Any good stories? Hmm, like a fairy tale? I'm not sure I know any of those off the top of my head."

"That's okay. Any story will do. Tell me something from your childhood. What do you remember?"

"Well, there was this one time my older brother told me about a haunted old barn on the outskirts of town. He said that his friend Jimmy's older brother had told Jimmy that a girl was murdered in that barn. This is a little dark actually, maybe I should think of something else."

Eve shook her head fervently and squeezed his hand, urging him to continue.

"Okay. So, Jimmy told him that the little girl had a brother that always kept an eye on her, but one day he kicked his ball a little too far down the street and ran after it. In the minute that he was gone, someone had come around and snatched up his sister. After he searched and searched through the whole town and couldn't find her he felt so guilt ridden that he went to the old barn to hide from his parents. He crawled up into the hayloft and looked down over the edge onto the barn floor. That's when he saw his sister's body laying lifeless in a pile of hay below."

Isaac paused to make sure the story hadn't upset his mother-in-law, but she was still smiling and rapt at attention. He took a breath and continued.

"My brother told me all of this under our family's porch one night. We had a little crawlspace that he and I liked to hide in. Our parents didn't know about it. He told me that when there's a full moon, if you crawled up into that hayloft at midnight and peered over the edge, just as her brother did, you could see the little girl's body looking back up at you."

"Oh, I've always loved a good ghost story. Tell me you tried it? Did you sneak into the barn at midnight?"

"Hold your horses, Eve," Isaac laughed, "I'm getting to that part. My brother dared me to go into the old barn during the next full moon and I, of course, couldn't say no to my older brother or else he'd make fun of me. I was scared out of my mind, but I put on a brave face. The next full moon happened a couple of days later. My brother and I snuck out of the house around eleven and met Jimmy at the old barn. They told me we all were going to climb into the hayloft and look over the edge together, but they made me go first. I was so frightened that I climbed the ladder as fast as I could without looking down and got to the top before realizing that my brother and Jimmy were not behind me. They never had any intention of climbing up there with me at all.

Before I could climb back down they had taken the ladder and I heard hysterical laughter coming from below me. They yelled, 'Look over the edge! Look down! Is she there? Can you see the ghost girl?' I was so angry with them, but if I didn't look then they would call me a wimp for weeks. So I got on my hands and knees and crawled to the edge of the hayloft and looked down. There, in a pile of hay below, was a body dressed in a white dress staring up at me. I screamed at the top of my lungs and jumped backwards away from the edge. That's when I heard more laughter coming from the pile of hay. Jimmy's brother had dressed up in one of their sister's dresses and laid in the hay to scare me."

Eve burst out laughing. She couldn't decide which was funnier, thinking about her son-in-law scared of a boy in a dress, or a boy in a dress.

"Boys are so cruel to each other sometimes. I feel so lucky that I was blessed with a little girl to raise. Whenever she was wearing a dress, she was supposed to be!"

"His sister was so angry when she found her dress the next day covered in hay and smelling like a barn, but not nearly as angry as my parents were when I told them what my brother had done."

"I can only imagine! I'm glad you have memories like that though. Life would be so boring if only easy and happy things happened to you. Sometimes I find those memories the fondest to look back on, even if they weren't so nice at the time."

"Do you have any memories like that, Eve?"

Eve smiled and patted Isaac's hand.

"A few, dear, but I won't bore you with them now," she said with a yawn before falling quickly to sleep. Isaac sat her for a while longer, watching the blankets rhythmically rise and fall as she slept peacefully, before going to Beth's room to rouse her for the next shift. Beth was already awake when he got there, reading a book in her bed. It was different from the one she was reading earlier.

In this book the heroine was on a long quest to reclaim the kingdom that was stolen from her at birth. It was one of Beth's favorites. She had already read it four, or five times, but she couldn't seem to focus on any other book. The girl in this story grew up without a family; she had been kidnapped as an infant. She only found out about the kingdom that she rightfully had claim to in a dream she had on her eighteenth birthday. An old fairy appeared inside the dream to tell her what she must do to reclaim the throne. According to the fairy, there were three trials, each one harder than the next. The girl didn't head the fairy's warning to face each test in the order she described and she was badly injured. But the fairy anticipated this. She had watched the girl since her birth and knew of her ambitious qualities. The fairy turned out to be her fairy godmother who helped her get well again and put her back on track. With her fairy godmother's help, the girl learned patience and successfully faced the three trials in order to win back her kingdom. Beth sometimes thought of her grandmother as her fairy godmother.

Beth sat at her grandmother's bedside holding the book on her lap and only pretending to read it. She mostly held on to the volume like a security blanket. She'd skim a few lines and then look up over the pages at Eve, still asleep. Every time she looked away she worried that her grandmother might have stopped breathing and she was unknowingly sitting in a room with a deceased person. This thought scared her. She loved her grandmother and wanted to be there for her in her time of need, but she couldn't shake the feeling that she could pass at any moment. Beth didn't want to be the person to find her grandmother that way and decided to end her shift early. She walked into her mother and father's room and tapped Sarah on the shoulder. Sarah turned over to face Beth.

"What's the matter?"

"I can't, Ma. I don't want to watch Nana die."

Beth began to cry.

"Shh, shh, sweatheart. It's all right. You don't have to. I know how scary it must be to think about. Don't worry. You go off to bed and I'll sit with Nan. You can come see her in the morning when we're all awake. How about that?"

Beth sniffled and nodded. She hugged her mother, collected her book, and went back to bed. It was too much to ask her children to sit alone with their ailing grandmother. She should have realized it sooner. Aaron might be able to handle it, but Beth was still so young. She didn't have any experience with death yet and it frightened her. Sarah wrapped a robe around herself and went to her mother's room. Eve was laying on her back with a peaceful expression on her face. Her hands were laced across her belly and she was almost perfectly still. Sarah's stomach dropped for a moment thinking that her mother had already passed until she saw the up and down movement of her chest. Sarah let out a sigh of relief and sat down in the chair next to her mother's bedside.

In the dim light, and all her muscles relaxed, Sarah could see a younger woman in her mother's face. When she was a child, she recalled watching her mother get ready in the mornings before church. Eve would run a comb through her deep chestnut hair until it shone like silk before pinning it in a bun behind her head. Sarah remembered wondering why her mother never wore her hair down; it was so beautiful that way. Eve didn't wear any makeup, but she'd pinch the apples of her cheeks to make them pink. When Sarah asked why she would do this, her mother replied, "Because it brings life to your face, and life is what makes a person beautiful." Then she'd reach down and lightly pinch Sarah's cheeks until she giggled.

Sarah reached over to stroke her sleeping mother's face. The gentle touch caused Eve's eyes to flutter open.

"Oh, hello, dear. You're not Isaac. I must have fallen asleep while we were chatting. How rude of me."

"Don't worry, Mama. He's fast asleep now. I'm sorry I woke you up."

"Don't be. I'll have plenty of time to sleep soon."

Sarah flinched at her mother's joke.

"Dear, don't be so sensitive. You knew this was coming."

"I knew it would come eventually. Aaron said six months. I thought I'd have time to prepare."

"And how would you do that? Slowly distance yourself from me over the next couple of months so that it hurt less when I passed? That doesn't seem like a better situation to me. No. I'd much rather things be as they are now."

"You're saying you wouldn't want more time?"

"I thought I did. When the doctors told me I only had six more months I thought, '*only* six more months? That gives me so much time to do the things I want to do before I go!' But I realized that I have already done everything I wanted to do. I fell in love with an amazing man, I raised a truly incredibly daughter, I was a part of my grandchildren's lives, I went skinny dipping in a pond! Anything else would be overkill. I'm happy with how my life turned out, how you turned out, I really am. I don't feel sad, dear. I feel so grateful to have done everything I wanted to do."

"Mama, I'm afraid I won't feel the same way when it's my turn to go. What if I've taken my husband for granted or didn't pay enough attention to my children? What if, when it's my turn, I'm sitting where you are now, but there's no one at my bedside?"

"My darling girl, the fact that you're thinking about that now means you have time to make sure it will never come true. You have a loving husband, with an amazing sense of humor might I add, at your side. Your children are caring and intelligent. Those are all things you had a hand in. That's the best thing about being a good wife and mother. The people you surround yourself are good, too. I don't see any future in which you end up alone. I raised you too well for an ending like that one."

Sarah got out of her chair and crawled into bed with her mother. Eve wrapped her daughter in a warm embrace and stroked her hair while she softly wept. Together, they hummed a lullaby that Eve and Eddie would sing to Sarah when she was a child. Sometime between the fourth or fifth rendition, mother and daughter fell asleep in each other's arms.

In the early hours of the morning, Aaron became restless when no one had come to collect him for his shift. He walked into the master bedroom to find his mother and grandmother sleeping soundly. He approached the bed and gently shook Sarah awake. She groggily opened her eyes and groaned in an attempt to prove she was alert.

"Ma, why don't you go back to bed with Pa. I'll take over sitting with Nan for the rest of the night."

Sarah groaned again, this time in agreement, and shuffled back to her room in a half asleep stupor. She failed to notice the well-worn, leather-bound book in her son's hands. Aaron had spent most of the night reading through his grandmother's diary. In his head, he referred to it as her diary because that's what she called it, but it was more than that. Eve had chronicled every event, good or bad, in her marriage and family life, and followed each one up with what she had learned from the experience. From moments as life changing as Sarah's birth, to things as trivial as an argument over breakfast, Eve had collected them all. Aaron didn't know if she had intended to create a complete encyclopedia of her adult life for others to read or not, but he felt like it would be a shame not to pass it on.

Sitting by her bedside, Aaron had almost read through the entirety of his grandmother's journal when he finally reached the final page. To his surprise, it was the only page in the whole book that Nana had left blank. What else could she possibly have left to add and would she have time to do it? Aaron became so nervous that this final page would stay forever empty if she were to pass before she had the time to write in it. He had to know what she intended to write. Aaron reached over and shook his grandmother awake.

"Nan, Nana, why is this last page blank? What were you saving it for?"

Eve slowly opened her eyes and yawned.

"Aaron, dear, what are you doing up? It has to be early morning by now."

"I'm not tired, Nan. I finished your diary. What are you going to write on the last page? It's the only unmarked page in the whole book."

"Nosy, just like your old Nan, except I like to think of it as being inquisitive. That page, I was saving that page for something special. I wouldn't want to spoil the ending for you."

"You're not going to tell me?"

"How about you let me finish the book and then you and your family can read it together, hm? Since you've already read most of it you'll be able to tell them what it's all about."

"Did you write this book for us?"

"Not at first. At first it was just a journal that my father gave me when I got married. He told me, 'Eve, you're not going to want to miss a thing, even the bad things. Write everything down so you can learn from the bad and repeat the good.' So I wrote down everything for myself. Only recently did I realize that what I'd actually done is write the origin story for your mother, you and your sister, and every Miller to follow."

"It's beautiful, Nan, it really is. I have something for you."

Aaron reached under his chair and pulled out a small, intricately carved box. A floral design covered the sides of the box and on the top Aaron had carved a perfect representation of her and Eddie's secret pond. Their initials were etched into the surface of the water. Aaron handed the box to his grandmother. Eve ran her fingers over the entire thing, feeling every nook and cranny. Her eyes filled with tears.

"Oh, Aaron, this is lovely. Is this what you've been working at your apprenticeship?"

"Yeah, I figured you be able to keep your knitting needles in it, or whatever else you would want to use it for."

"Sweetheart, this is an amazing gift. Thank you. I will cherish it for as long as I'm alive and then some. I'm sure you read about the pond in my diary, but what made you choose it, out of all the other things and places I described, to carve?"

"There were times in your writing that you went out of your way to say 'This made me happy,' but whenever you wrote about the pond, you didn't need to point it out. That feeling just came through naturally."

Eve looked at her grandson with wonderment. She had truly never met someone as emotionally in tune as him. Her family would be left in very capable hands once she was gone. She needn't worry about that.

"There's no one on God's green earth like you, dear. Don't ever forget that."

Aaron took the box from her hands and replaced it with his. He carefully squeezed her small fingers and then let go. The diary balanced precariously on the edge of the bed. He picked it up and handed it to her.

"I'll stay with you while you finish it. I won't peek, I promise!"

"Very well, dear. I think it's about time I finally finish this book, hm?"

Aaron placed a pencil into his grandmother's outstretched hand and leaned back to make a show of not looking at the page while she wrote. Eve sat there for a moment, not writing a word, before she put the tip of the pencil to the page. Aaron expected her to go on for a while, carefully curating the final passage of her memoir, but it took her only a few strokes of her pencil and no time at all to finish.

"That's it?"

"That's it."

"You don't have anything more to say than that?"

"How do you know I didn't say a lot?"

"You wrote a single word! Maybe two."

"Dear, you're confusing quality with quantity. This is what I wanted to say and I said it. Write your own book if you're not happy with it."

Aaron was dismayed. He worried that his grandmother's final words wouldn't be enough to comfort him once she passed. It was not fair of him to put that burden on her, he knew, but he desperately wanted to know that he'd be able to learn something new from her when she wasn't there.

"My dearest grandson, I'm afraid you've built me up to be some wise old sage, but I'm just your grandmother. I'm just me."

Aaron nodded and relaxed some. He trusted his grandmother.

"Why don't you go to bed and get some rest. You look exhausted. I'll be fine until morning."

"No way, Nan. I'll be here wide awake all night," he let out a yawn," but maybe I'll rest my eyes just for a moment."

Aaron crossed his arms, leaned back in the chair, and closed his eyes. Eve watched him sleep for a little while before closing her eyes herself. When Aaron woke up after the sun rose the next morning Nan's eyes were still closed, a smile still on her face. She had passed away painlessly as he slept. Eve had ended her story exactly where she had begun it, in her old family home surrounded by love.

***

Their family held a small service in the graveyard where Grandpa Eddie was buried. A headstone had been etched and placed on the plot directly next to his. It read, "Eve Miller, Beloved Daughter, Wife, Mother, and Grandmother." Sarah had fussed about what should be written on it, but Aaron insisted on keeping it simple.

"This was exactly what Nan set out to be," he said, "we should honor that."

They buried her with the wooden box Aaron made her, her knitting needles, and a pair of Eddie's socks that had little cups of coffee printed on them. They found the pair when they went through her things. Beth thought it might be nice to include the diary, but Aaron told her what was inside. The story wasn't Nan's anymore, it was theirs. He still couldn't bring himself to read the last page yet. He didn't know what he was waiting for.

Sarah had already been wearing black since her father's funeral, but Isaac changed his clothes to match his wife, and their children followed suite. Aaron prepared himself for a year of everyone in his house wearing black. He understood that it was tradition, but didn't know if he could handle seeing such a literal representation of gloom for twelve whole months. He confided this in his father and the next day Isaac tapped him on the shoulder and lifted his pant leg to reveal a colorful knit sock. It had come from the bag of knitting Eve had left them.

"Don't tell your mother, but I've left a pair in your room as well. Your Nana wouldn't want us to mope around for an entire year. This way we can keep a little joyful piece of her with us, while still showing our respect. Just wear your pants a little long."

Aaron hugged his father tight. He was right. Nan wouldn't have supported this extended period of mourning. When Grandpa Eddie died she wore a polka dot dress to his funeral, much to the dismay of Sarah. When Aaron asked her why she wasn't dressed for mourning she insisted that she was.

"Grandpa Eddie and I promised that we wouldn't wear black to each other's funeral. He reasoned that there would be so many people dressed all in black that he wouldn't be able to pick me out of the crowd when he looked down on us from heaven. He made me promise that I'd wear polka dots, that way he'd be able to spot me right away, and if I were to pass first I insisted he wear a lime green suit. I'm heartbroken to say goodbye to Eddie for a number of reasons, one being that I'll never get to see him in that suit."

After the funeral, the family returned to their home in solemn silence. Isaac made coffee while Sarah sat at the kitchen table and Beth immediately locked herself in her bedroom. Aaron had only told his sister about Nana's diary, but even she hadn't read it yet. He didn't like the fact that his family was acting like Nan was gone for good so he decided to show them the book. He went to his room to fetch the memoir and pulled Beth out of her hideout on the way. They sat down at the kitchen table across from their mother and Aaron placed the diary in the center. Sarah looked at it curiously.

"What's this, Aaron?"

"It's Nan's diary. Wrote in it almost every day since the day she married Grandpa Eddie. You're in it. We're all in it, but mostly Nan's in it. Everything important that she ever did or learned is written in this book and she left it here for us."

Sarah placed one hand over her mouth. After being so angry with Eve for giving her unsolicited advice, she almost felt guilty for the rush of joy she felt upon seeing that book filled with her mother's words. It took her a few minutes but eventually she worked up the courage to pick up her mother's diary and flip open the front cover. Hesitantly, she began to read but picked up the pace as she went on. Sarah read her mother's memoir voraciously, reading every word of every story. Starting with the awkward tale of her wedding night, quiet moments in the middle of the night when Eve had to rock baby Sarah back to sleep, and ending with their fight, Sarah read it all.

One particular story stuck out to her. It was when Sarah was nine years old and feisty as ever. Eve recounted a time when she had taken her daughter with her to the market. Sarah pouted the whole way there because she'd rather have stayed home and chased the chickens. Eddie was out in the fields so there was no one around to watch her, but Sarah tried to convince her mother that she was old enough to take care of herself. "I'm nine," she reasoned, but Eve wouldn't budge. Once they got to the market however, Sarah began to soften. She enjoyed helping her mother pick out food and other things to buy. Eve even let her give the money over to the tender.

The walk home was completely different than the walk there. They chatted about how much Sarah liked to buy things and how excited she was to have money of her own someday. Then Eve explained to her how one made money and she got even more excited. Eve wrote all about that day in vibrant detail. Sarah was expecting the story to resolve in some sort of life lesson, but all her mother had to say about the shopping trip was how happy she was that she got to spend those moments with her daughter. This simple moment meant enough to Eve to record it, and now it was something Sarah could cherish as well.

Aaron had sat with his mother all day as she read, waiting for her to get to that final page. Isaac tried to convince him to do other things, at least get up from the table and move around, but he wouldn't budge. He wanted to know what his grandmother had written and he wanted to find out with his mother, so he sat across from her waiting patiently while she read. When she finally had flipped to the second to last page he told her to stop.

"Nan wrote something very important on that final page. I watched her do it. I don't know what it was but she was very insistent that we wait until she passed over to read it. I just thought you should know that before we find out what it says."

Sarah nodded to her son to show that she understood and flipped the page. The next sheet was mostly blank except for three small words in Nana's handwriting scrawled across the center. The page said, *"Book one of ?"*

"Book one of question mark?" Sarah asked incredulously, "What is that supposed to mean?"

Sarah was confused, but Aaron understood right away. The book that Nan had written wasn't just her story, it was all of theirs, and Eve's life wasn't just her own, it belonged to her family. Every story she wrote down, everything she learned influenced each of them in some way. This book didn't mark the end of her life, it was only the beginning. It was up to them to carry on her legacy, their legacy, and to make sure the story never had an ending.

Aaron explained all of this to his Sarah, who cried then for the last time about her mother's death. She then remembered something eve had said after her father's funeral. When she angrily confronted her about why she refused to wear mourning clothes Eve responded by saying, "What's the point in dying if everyone else can't go on living?" Sarah didn't understand at the time, the cryptic quote only made her more frustrated, but now she finally understood. After giving Aaron a big hug, Sarah walked to her room, changed into a plain linen dress, and put on a kettle of tea.

AMISH WISHES

JESSICA PENN

1.

Tracing her finger over the cold, gray tombstone, Joanna inhaled deeply and choked back a sob. Kneeling in the pasture of their family's cemetery, she placed a bouquet of daffodils in front of the stone. It all felt like a dream to her. She didn't think she would ever lose her mother. She was her best friend and now that she was gone Joanna felt lost. She spoke softly to the stone just as she would as if her mother were standing beside her. "Hello, Mother. I miss you more each day. I really wish you could have stayed. It's lonely here without you. Everyone is trying to be strong. They want to continue life as it was before, but without you being here, it's impossible. I know you're in a better place and you're not in pain from the illness ravaging your earthly body, but it's still hard. I just don't know what to do now. I have assumed all of your household duties, just as you would have wished, but I find myself feeling increasingly empty. None of this feels right." Before she could finish her conversation, she heard the distinctive sound of horses clopping in the distance. She knew her brothers would be coming to take her back to their small home in the center of their community. They would have finished their errands in town, and she would be needed soon to start preparing supper. Dusk would be upon them soon, and after evening services, a good meal, a nice fire, and sleep would be arriving soon.

Joanna stood up slowly and ran her fingers along the cold stone one more time, giving a weak smile of recognition to her brother, Eli, who trotted up on his prized horse, Petunia. Petunia was a gentle creature and was easily broken. Eli was good to the creature and she respected him as well, she wouldn't ever buck him off, even when they were traveling through thunderstorms or if she ran up on a snake in the tall weeds. They trusted one another. Joanna could say the same about her brother, even though she was the older sibling, they trusted one another and vowed to always protect one another through all of life's trials. Eli looked down from Petunia and frowned. He hated to see his sister suffer so, but as a young man, he knew that for the good of the community he couldn't let his own sorrows show. He had to be strong for his sister now and show nothing but unconditional support. Now was the time for them to come together as a family and keep each other close. That's what his mother would have wanted. "It's good to see you, sister. Are you ready to return to the house?"

Joanna looked up at Eli's eyes and knew that behind the deep brown spheres, there was a touch of sadness that lingered there. He was trying so hard to put on a brave front, but she knew the truth, he wouldn't be the same after their mother's passing either. "Yes. I'm ready to return, Eli. Can I ride with you?"

"Of course. I think Petunia has it in her to walk us both back home along the path." The horse merely whinnied and they both laughed at her response. As they trotted along the path, Joanna's voice turned solemn once again as she asked, "How's father today?"

"He didn't say much at all, he merely got up and went into his study, where he read some scriptures and made some notes for service, then he walked out into the garden and surveyed the crops. It was like a typical day for him it seems."

"I wish he would express himself more."

"Ah, you know how he is Joanna, that's how he always was, stoic and stone-faced."

"Yeah. Maybe one day we'll figure him out."

"Ha! You have jokes, my sister. I seriously have my doubts about that."

They rode back up to the house in relative silence only listening to the sounds of the birds chirping and the echo of Petunia's hooves against the ground. Reaching the house, the pair dismounted and Eli walked Petunia to the barn, taking care to make sure she had plenty of fresh hay and water. Joanna went straight into the house and immediately made her way to the kitchen. In her mind's eye, she could still see her mother standing by the stove, stirring a pot or leaning over to get a knife from the bottom drawer. It was up to her now to make sure the family was fed. She sighed heavily and reached up above the family's ice box to take down a larger pot which hung above it. It was cast iron and the same one that had been used in the family for generations to make hearty stews and soups. That night Joanna decided she would make the family a hearty beef stew. They had some extra meat frozen already in the icebox and she had plenty of canned vegetables from the summer and fall's gardening. She poured some water that had already been carried inside into the large cast iron pot and lit the fire beneath their wood and coal stove. When it came to a full boil she added the meat and vegetables. Her mother had always tried to make her stews last for a few days and made it a point to ensure it was filling as well. Joanna added some corn starch to thicken the broth and proceeded to flavor it with spices. When her father walked into the kitchen, he hung his head, but then looked up and met Joanna's eyes, giving her a slight nod of approval. When the preparations were finished Joanna carried the pot along with some freshly baked bread out to the dining room. The family took their assigned places around the square table. In their mourning period, it was customary to set an extra place at the table for the lost as well, so her mother's chair while empty next to her father, had a place setting and was served some stew as well. It would be her father's task to consume it.

2.

After all was seated, her father spoke. "Good evening my son and daughter. Let us all rejoice and give thanks for what the day hath brought forth. Now is the time we must graciously give thanks for the abundance the Lord hath provided us with and draw close together as a family in our hour of need. I was reading the scriptures this morning and they brought me much comfort. Despite our loss, I trust each of my children to go on living and continue to be upstanding and show true grace. Now let us break bread and honor the fallen."

They all opened their eyes and lifted their heads watching their father who broke the first bit of bread. He then passed the plate to the others who took their portions and set the tray back in the center of the table. Their meal was eaten in silence and no one dared to speak until their simple supper was finished. Their father then looked at each of them and smiled. Tufts of white hair showed his age and he had a natural ruddiness to his skin tone that made him look jovial. He also had lines etched along his forehead left by the many years of being contemplative. One would look at him and assume he was a stern man all of the time, but he had crows feet and smile lines along his eyelids that told another story. While their father was stern and quiet, Joanna could remember a time when they were children he would play their games with them and tell stories which made all of them laugh joyously. He was a man dedicated to worship, but he also was a man who prided himself on the family he had created.

Rising from the table Joanna began to gather the dishes and place them in the kitchen sink, as she crossed into the other room she heard her father say, "Joanna, I'm very pleased with all the progress you have made in the kitchen with meal preparations. Your mother, rest her soul, would be very proud of you." Tears formed in Joanna's eyes and she bit her bottom lip to choke back a sob. Her mother, Annabelle, had been gone now for over a month, but the loss still stung. Her entire family was stuck living with the reminders of her being. Joanna still hadn't had the heart to clean out her closet or her sewing room. The elders had planned a town gathering at the end of the month, however, so she thought she would take them then and donate them. After all, she was a practical woman, just like her mother before her, and knew that there was no sense in good pieces of clothing going to waste when someone less fortunate could be using them. She responded to her father when returning to the table for a second trip for the remainder of the dishes. "Thank you father, I appreciate it. I discover more techniques every day. I feel personal growth is important, don't you?"

"Why, of course it is, Joanna. I've watched you and Eli grow through the years and I'm proud of both of you. I personally feel comforted by the fact that no matter how many times I go to complete a task and fail, I always have another opportunity to give it another try. That's the beauty in salvation and forgiveness. As humans, we all fall short of perfection, but there's always the chance to redeem yourself through prayer and multiple attempts."

Eli cleared his throat and spoke for the first time since they arrived home. "I'm glad for that. I know that there have been many times I felt lost or like I was on the wrong path, but I would pray about it and then something would happen or suddenly change in my life." Joanna listened to the pair talk from the kitchen while washing up the supper dishes and smiled. She loved her father and brother dearly but felt lost. She had no one to talk about her daily affairs with now that her mother had passed. She couldn't tell her father about the gossip she overheard while getting notions for sewing. She couldn't talk to her brother about a certain feeling she had in the pit of her stomach when she watched the baker's son splitting wood while hanging their linens out to dry.

She listened as their conversation continued. Her father spoke in a good-natured tone and there was nothing condescending in his voice as he elaborated on the subject matter with his son. "Eli, do you remember that time you came home crying when you were thirteen or fourteen? It was late in the evening and mid-summer. You had just returned from Mrs. Hollister's barn dance, she was having to raise money for the local town orphanage. You came to me and had tears in your eyes and your lips were swollen and shaking. I'll never forget how dejected you looked."

"Yes, father. I remember that well. I had gone to the dance and got quite upset when I saw Pamela Davison dancing with my friend, James."

"Do you remember what I told you?"

"No, I can't say I can recall, though it must have worked, I haven't harbored feelings for Pamela since that night."

"What I told you then son, was that sometimes we think we know what's best for ourselves, but in the end, it's not us who is ultimately in control of that. Our actions may influence our day to day activities, but it is only through faith we can fulfill our ultimate destiny. Our almighty father wants us to be happy, but sometimes we have to learn a lesson the hard way so we don't pursue other things. Your courtship with Pamela, for example, is one of those things. Do you know what she's doing now?"

"No, father. I haven't a clue."

"She decided to go live among the outsiders. Her life has not been beneficial from it, given my understanding. The last news we received in a letter that she decided to pursue her career as a professional dancer. It turns out that career path led her to work in a nightclub for exotic dancing and she's developed a drug addiction. It's in my best estimation that she will more than likely spend a great deal of her life in prison for drug related crimes or prostitution. So, son, as you can see sometimes our Father doesn't answer our prayers for a reason."

"What if I could have changed her? If she stayed with me, then maybe she would have just lived her life pursuing the path of righteousness."

"Well, I know how susceptible young men are to the wiles of women and their charms. I think that given the choice, you would have left and gone with her and been corrupted by the outside world as well. Outside of our community, there is a temptation to pursue wrongdoing on every corner. No matter what your vice, there is some way to purchase it or attain it there. Never forget that on your travels, Eli."

"I won't Father."

3.

Joanna listened to their conversation while she continued to tidy up the dinner dishes. She knew that her mother would have loved that their father was attempting to socialize with his children, but she also knew that her mother would have played devil advocate in the conversation. She wasn't like most of the other women in the town. She was outspoken and often had heated debates on matters of faith or business with her father, yet they worked to balance each other out very well. Joanna was convinced that when God made her mother, his creation was done purely to spite her father and keep him in line.

She cleaned up the sink and then decided she would go ahead and get the percolator ready for the morning's coffee. She knew that would be the first thing their father would ask for when he woke up in the morning. He often preferred the strong brew first thing, then would go out to complete his chores, foregoing breakfast until their animals had been fed. He always said that if one took care of the animals, they would, in turn, take care of you. He lived by this strict routine day in and day out, with little variation in routine, save for the day he celebrated his wedding anniversary with his wife. On that day, both their father and mother would take a rare trip to town, where they would return with not only small gifts for the children but some goods, that were less costly to purchase such as new blades for the farming equipment. Joanna always dreamed of the outside world as being some type of magical realm where everyone had access to things like running water and life was easy, but as she grew older she realized the outsiders weren't much different than those in her own community. She wasn't allowed to do much traveling into town, but when she did she just noticed that the outsiders seemed to base their own value on their material belongings. This concept just simply didn't exist in her community, everything was shared.

Joanna saw that it was dark now outside and with her chores attended to, she didn't see the point in staying with the menfolk talking around the dinner table. Drying her hands on a dish towel, she decided to go ahead and excuse herself. Walking around the side of the table she approached her father and placed her hand on the side of his chair then leaned over kissing him on the forehead. "I'm going to go ahead and turn in for the evening, father. The nightly chores are all completed."

"Ah, yes, very good little one. My precious daughter. You have sweet dreams and remember that your father and brother are here if you have night terrors."

"Oh, papa. I love you. I haven't had a night terror, though, since I was seven years old."

"Still.. think good thoughts."

"I will. Goodnight. Goodnight Eli."

"Goodnight, sister, remember I love you even in your slumber."

"I will."

Joanna walked to her bedroom and lit the small candle that was on her nightstand, it provided enough light to read by, which is the only thing she enjoyed doing in the evenings to relax. Taking off her bonnet, she sat on the edge of the bed and began undoing the long braids she had in her hair. She preferred to keep it pulled up and away from her face during the course of the day since she was often doing chores. The tresses undid themselves easily and she fluffed hands through it, taking her hairbrush and running it through her long brown locks. After she put on her nightgown and hung her daytime dress back up in her standing closet, she picked up her Bible, seeing the notes she had made in the margins. She had been studying a chapter in Revelations that her father recommended. He felt that it would benefit the family to examine the reasons for death together, so they could make some sense of their mother's unexpected passing. She sighed and remembering her place decided she would finish reading and analyzing the chapter when she arose the following morning. Instead, she picked up the paperback she had borrowed from the town's library. It had a handsome cowboy on the front of it and he appeared in front of a herd of galloping horses. He was holding a blonde woman in his arms and she was swooning. Joanna smiled as the opened the book to the place she left off. It wasn't customary for women in her community to read much at all, but she enjoyed the thoughts of romance and found nothing wrong with dreaming about a handsome cowboy of her own. She finished the chapter and blew out her candle, reclining on her twin bed and closing her eyes sleeping almost immediately.

4.

As the dawn peeked through the clouds, Joanna was awakened by Eli, barging into her bedroom unannounced. He let the door bang on the hinges and had a panicked look on his face, as Joanna pulled the covers up over herself asked, "Why, Eli?! Whatever is the matter?! Is it Father?! Is he okay?!"

"Yes. Oh, Joanna, I'm worried. It's Petunia. She's fallen ill I'm afraid. Can you come out to the barn?"

Breathing out a sigh of relief, Joanna nodded and said, "Of course dear brother. Don't be fearful. The Lord will protect Petunia. Give me a few moments to get decent and I will be out there." Joanna calmly got up from her bed and walked to her closet, taking a few moments to pull her hair back and put on her bonnet then putting on her daytime dress. She pulled the laces tight on her boots and hurried out to the barn where she could see Eli standing by Petunia's stall pacing anxiously. "Thank you for coming out sister. I can't figure out what's wrong with her. She won't respond to my coaxing and she's just lethargic. I've never seen her in this state."

"Calm yourself, Eli. Your panicked state is doing her no good either. Animals can sense your fear." Joanna walked up to the mare who was laying down and looked into Petunia's deep brown eyes. She then placed her hand gently on the creature's forehead. She then stroked the animal's head and back, making soothing sounds, just as her mother would do them when they were sick youngsters. "Yes. You're right to have come to fetch me. She's definitely fallen ill. Let's just hope its a bug. Father has a trip planned to go into town to gather some new ax blades for the fall cutting. I'll go with him and stop by the library and see if I can find a cure in some of the veterinary medicine books they have shelved. Don't worry, brother. We will do what we can for her. Just be fervent in your prayers and there will be a way delivered."

Joanna walked back into the home and began preparing her father's morning coffee. Daylight had just broke and she knew he would be happy to get the day started like normal. When he walked in the kitchen he smiled seeing her standing at the stove as her mother would have, fixing his coffee and preparing breakfast for her brother. Eli always had a voracious appetite She set the steaming mug in front of him and said, "Good morning, Father. I must confess it's already been eventful."

"Oh, really how so?"

"It seems Petunia has fallen ill. I was hoping it would be okay if I went with you while you were in town today to look up some medicine for her at the library."

"I certainly hate to hear that Petunia has taken a turn for the worse. She has been good to our little family. I think that's a wonderful idea darling. God can work miracle cures, but only if we're willing to do a bit of the work as well. After the morning feeding, we will go into town. Be prepared. While I'm purchasing the new blades for the fall wood harvest, you can look into a cure for our Petunia. I bet your brother is worried sick."

"Oh, he is Father. You know he's always been close to the mare."

"We shall do what we can. Thank you for the finely brewed cup of coffee. Now I must get to work, the daylight is already streaming upon us and the chickens will be happy to receive their breakfast."

"Thank you, Father."

Joanna finished making the biscuits and gravy for breakfast then poured them all glasses of freshly squeezed orange juice from the assortment of oranges that they had traded for in town earlier in the summer. She knew their shelf life would be expiring soon and didn't want anything to go to waste. Waste not, want not, her mother always said. She also knew that they all need to keep their strength up because as soon as they got back from town the entire community would gather and chop wood for their collective heat in the winter. After completing her chores and cleaning up the cooking utensils she set the meal on the dining room table and gathered her bag for their trip into town. She made certain she had her city library card and decided to take her paperback with her and exchange it for another as it was nearing completion anyway. Looking around the empty room she sighed. She was worried about her brother, but also she felt a doubt creeping into her soul and a generalized discomfort, wondering if this is how the remainder of her days would be spent, taking care of her father and brother , never knowing the love of a man or having her own family to raise.

Her father and brother came back into the house after feeding the animals and sat down at the table, nodding in appreciation at having their meal already set before them. Eli spoke then, asking to say the morning prayers and included a blessing for his favorite mare as well. They ate the rest of their meal in silence and Joanna immediately went to the sink and began cleaning up the dishes, so she wouldn't have to do both the breakfast and dinner dishes before bed. She also was anticipating having a busy day tending to Petunia upon their return. Her father came and got her when the horses were hitched up to the wagon and her brother helped her climb in beside him. Her father gave his horses a quick pat on the head and they departed on their journey into town.

5.

Arriving in the nearest town, Joanna took in her surroundings as her father hitched up the wagon to the hitching post by the hardware store. She got out of the buggy, amidst the stares of the townspeople. She imagined she looked quite strange to then in her pale blue day dress, with her hair pinned up in a bonnet, while her father was dressed head to toe in all black, complete with his wide-rimmed black hat. His long brown beard wasn't shaved, merely groomed and it did betray his age, as spots of gray could be seen in it when the sun hit it just right. He spoke briefly to his daughter before going inside the store. "Remember daughter, be polite to the townspeople, but do not engage in lengthy conversation unless it pertains to spreading the Gospel. I will be here when you are ready to leave but try to find the information you seek quickly. I suspect this lost time will hurt our productivity later and we won't be able to get as much done as we should. Be careful, Joanna."

Joanna nodded and hugged her father before crossing the street and rounding the block heading to the library. She cast her eyes downward mostly only looking up periodically to dodge obstacles. She opened the doors to the city library and the pleasant librarian smiled and waved at her when she entered. She smiled back and returned the greeting. She liked the librarian, who never questioned her when she came in even as a little girl clutching her mother's skirts. The older clerk would give her lollipops when her mother checked out her religious books and romance novels. Now Joanna was grown and even though she didn't get a lollipop, she still felt those warm feelings when she was in the library. She walked up to the desk and quietly dropped her book on the counter. "I need to return this, and I will be getting another one if I can find the other information I need in time."

"Sure thing, Joanna. Have you been doing okay, since your mother's passing?"

"Oh, yes we have been doing alright, thank you. I'm sorry I was in such a bad state when you saw me last. I am adjusting to this new normal."

"Well, that's good. If you need anything, you let me know as always."

"I will. I will see you when I return."

Joanna then walked off, smiling once more at the clerk. She rounded the corner to the reference desk where there was no clerk, but there was a younger looking man in grease-stained coveralls standing by the finance books, looking bewildered. Joanna watched him pull out a book from the shelf as the rest came tumbling down. She couldn't stifle a small giggle as he fumbled trying to catch them all. He turned around hearing her laughter and she was met with a sheepish smile and the most striking blue eyes she'd ever seen. He took her by surprise as she felt her heart beat faster within her chest and suddenly heat rose to her face as she blushed deeply. Before she could say a word he smiled broadly at her and said, "They don't make these shelves the way they used to do they?"

Joanna giggled once again and said, "No. They certainly don't."

"I don't really know much about this place. I needed a book on taxes, I own my own mechanic shop and I'm doing my own this year to save money for the business. Maybe I should have just paid someone."

"Well, what are you looking for? Maybe I can help."

"A book to tell me how to do it."

Joanna paused for a moment surveying the shelves then reached down to the bottom one, accidently brushing the man's hand as she picked up a hefty volume and placed it in his arms. "Here you go. This will guide you through the process."

"Oh wow. Thank you. I appreciate that ma'am. It's nice to meet you, my name's David."

"I'm Joanna. I'm not from around here, as you can tell."

David took a step toward her, closing the distance, and Joanna felt a certain electricity pass through them. She let the heat rise to her cheeks again and once more looked into his blue eyes. He was in good shape and looked strong from his work. He had blonde hair and was clean shaven. He didn't look like any of the men from their community, but he did seem to possess the same kindness behind his eyes and good spirit. He responded by saying, "I wish you were from around here. I'd hire you to do my taxes."

She chuckled at his joke, then suddenly remembered her purpose. "I really hate to cut on conversation short, David, but I have to get some information then return to my community, my brother's horse is sick and needs medical attention I know nothing of."

"Oh, I'm sorry to hear that. Maybe I can help. I grew up on a ranch."

She couldn't believe her ears. She had wanted a cowboy all of her own. Could it be that her prayers had been answered? He seemed so genuine and caring. She explained the problem with Petunia and David gave her the information she needed to attend to the mare. He reassured her it was nothing major that some tender loving care couldn't fix. He then went on to say that his specialty in life was fixing broken things. Joanna considered the gravity of his statement before turning to leave and decided to do something she would need to ask forgiveness for later.

"You have been so helpful David, could I have your address?"

"Only if I can have yours too."

The pair exchanged addresses and Joanna exited the library, turning around to see David staring at her making her exit. She didn't know what had come over her, but she knew in her heart this man was her destiny.

6.

She exited the library to find her father standing red-faced by the door, checking his pocket watch. She hadn't realized how much time had passed talking with David, she only knew that it felt like they had known each other a lifetime. Feeling the need to apologize she spoke to her father, when they crossed to the buggy, "I'm sorry, father. It took me longer to get the information I needed than what I thought."

He didn't say anything, but merely nodded and coaxed the horses out of the lot and towards the path back to their community. Her father finally spoke when they were close to the halfway point between town and their village. "You know why we caution each other when talking with townspeople? It's not because our religion has restrictions on being social and making friends. In fact, we are encouraged to witness to everyone we possibly can. It's because not all people are righteous, Joanna. Not everyone will have your best interest at heart, and the original evil does find its way into the hearts of men. Some of the people you encounter in the outside world, well let's say the majority of them, only are interested in preying on the weak. It's their life's goal, not helping others or doing good."

Joanna turned her eyes downward again as her father patted her on the leg continuing, "Remember, no matter what happens, Joanna, your family will always support you within the community. We, however, could not help you should you decide to live among the outsiders. You would be shunned and on your own, you know it's our way, there's no changing that." Joanna nodded in acknowledgment, silently rubbing the piece of paper in her pocket which had David's address on it. She knew in her heart, that she needed to see the mysterious cowboy mechanic once again, but didn't like the idea of her father's disapproval. He would never allow such a thing, she felt conflicted and sick at heart the entire way home.

Arriving back at the community they were greeted by Eli, whose worried look had only grown more exasperated during their time away. "Greetings, Father. Greetings, Sister. Did you acquire the knowledge you sought?"

"I did brother. Let's go to the barn and see what we can do."

Together they walked to the barn and checked on Petunia. Joanna took care to follow David's precise instructions and administered a careful mixture of salt brine and water to the mare who greedily lapped it up. It had seemed that she had just gotten a bit dehydrated during their previous days' activities and was feeling under the weather. They monitored her condition throughout the day and it did improve as she eventually got up and started wandering back and forth in her stall, anxious for a trot. In addition to that the new blade purchase, expedited the wood cutting process and the community made short work of the wood pile, stockpiling enough wood to last the entire winter in half the time it normally would. They decided as a community to celebrate their recent accomplishment and give thanks to the Lord, with a feast to be held that upcoming Saturday night.

Joanna spent the night quietly in her room after supper and allowed herself to think of David. She knew beyond a shadow of a doubt that she needed him in her life. She believed, despite her father's warnings that there were good and decency in his soul. No one without a good heart, would have freely given her that information she needed to help her animal. Most of the outsiders would have offered their services and charged a pretty penny for such knowledge. Joanna thought of the feast Saturday and sighed. Did she want to be stuck in the community all her life, eventually marrying a man who had little passion for anything in life? It was then Joanna made her decision. She would slip away during the barn dance on Saturday and go see David.

As the community was abuzz with the festivities at the dance on Saturday night, Joanna excused herself to go back to the house, hugging her brother and her father tightly before exiting, saying she felt ill and needed to call it an early night. Unnoticed by anyone else in the community, she then proceeded down the well-worn path and made her way to town. She made her way to the address David had scrawled on a ripped piece of an envelope from his coveralls and knocked on his door.

David opened the door, rubbing his eyes, apparently awakened by her rapping. He was groggy but smiled broadly in recognition. "Joanna, is that you are am I dreaming?"

"No. You're not dreaming, David. I'm really here." She paused a moment, considering her options. She thought for a moment about what advice her mother would give her in this moment. She thought back to when she was a little girl clutching on to her mother's skirt, frightened by some imaginary threat. She would have said, "Ah, my precious little girl, there is nothing to be afraid of but your own imagination. If you don't give your fear power over you, you can achieve anything you want in this lifetime." Joanna hesitated a moment then said to David all while blushing and smiling, "I came to be with you David, and hopefully one day be your wife."

David took Joanna by the hand and led her over his front stoop, making sure she didn't trip over the door sill on the way in. When he shut the door behind her he pulled her into his arms and kissed her deeply. Joanna felt a joy like none other she had felt in her life, spread through her bones and body. He then looked deeply into her eyes and said, "Well. I'm not the smartest man you will ever know, nor will I ever be the ideal of perfection, but I promise you this Joanna. I am a decent man with a good heart, and I promise to make this life the best we can possibly have together. So, yes. I do want you to stay with me. You're all I've thought about since I met you that day at the library, and you're all I want to think about for the rest of my days." The pair then walked hand in hand into David's modest living room where they sit side by side on the sofa, holding each other until they drifted off peacefully.

AMISH GOODNIGHT

GILLIAN BROWN

Chapter 1

Mary smiled, luxuriating in the warm sunlight as it danced across her pale skin, with her hand pressed firmly to her belly. Her normal Amish clothes had been traded-in for those which could easily accommodate a swelling stomach, and life felt purposeful and easy.

One of the beauties of Amish life, was the miracle of new birth. Yet, there were secrets around women's bodies within her community too. The older women often muttered around a female, prescribing all kinds of herbs and salves for whatever ailed her. Mary wanted to learn how to make these mysterious pastes, but was told quite pointedly that healing work was the business of older women, and she was far too young to take it on.

While English women held baby showers and gatherings before the birth of a new child, the Amish felt it best not to draw too much attention. After all, being in the spotlight was a form of pride. That, of course, and there was the fact that someone within her community was almost always with-child. Birthing did not carry the same stigmas in her world as it did in the English one.

Amish women would regularly work right up until the hour of their child's delivery. The lack of television and modern media meant that all the women had little to no exposure to the fact that many modern women feared the pain of birth, as well as complications during labor.

Within their communities there were significantly lower incidences of caesarian births, as well as pregnancy complications. Instead, they were surrounded by stories about easy childbirth and knew that labor was simply a normal part of life. New life was not something to be feared or even celebrated to excess. Instead, this was a mere fact of life.

Mary breathed deeply. Her husband Jacob should have been home already, but it wasn't terribly unusual for him to be late, especially since the busy season for their store was approaching. He was probably still building a shed or a shelf, toiling in the carpentry area of the shop, or maybe even huddled down, intently designing a crib for their new arrival.

Granted, Mary was only a few weeks along, but Jacob had been delighted when she'd told him the news. Like most Amish men, he'd been dreaming of having a son since he was a teenager. The idea that it might finally come to pass this year was a notion that swelled his heart with pride. A boy would be able to carry on the family name and traditions. Jacob would be able to pass on his carpentry skill set, and would grow old knowing their Amish lineage was secure.

Jacob was a simple man, who typically didn't want much from life. His parents, aunts, and uncles had helped the young couple to build their own store, which their community had cobbled together near the highway. There, they sold canned goods, vegetables, and other items made from wood like sheds and furniture.

Mary had been moved beyond words when Jacob's father had presented them the deed to their land. The rise in the cost of land in the English world had meant that so many of the Amish had no choice but to sell off their farms and move to Indiana where prices were significantly cheaper.

Lancaster county Pennsylvania had become impossibly expensive. The English world was one where capitalism reigned supreme, which meant that the Amish were left fumbling to try and preserve a way of life that was quickly going extinct.

Young couples who'd worked at manual labor their entire lives could no longer afford to buy even a few acres of land when they became of age. Yet, their culture was based-off farming and living off the land.

The Amish within her sect were never city dwellers, and so the availability of land had become a real problem. Many of the Amish had been forced into bankruptcy, which their preacher had referred to as another of the devil's works. After all, only in an evil society would good and hard-working folks fall so far behind.

Yet, the Amish way was one of peace. There would be no demonstrations to try and change the English world or reduce the surrounding s of land. There would be no complaints about the sheer unfairness of it all as they were being pushed out of their communities by the new high cost of living. They'd simply pray together and ask that God help them find a way.

As a result of the new market, Amish families now routinely banded together to help fund one another's land. The older generation understood that without their help, many young people would have no choice but to leave the Amish forever or starve on farms which yielded little crops because of poor location and over-farmed land. In order to survive, they had to band together.

The roadside store had been a great idea, and Mary and Jacob had been lucky. Their small plot of land was near the highway, and so the English were constantly driving by. Their curiosity about the Amish way of life made them want to stop in for cookies and pies—something Mary was happy to provide. Very often, they'd offer her bits of news about the outside world, information she both feared and relished.

The English would pull up in their expensive vans and cars, and most of them would stroll through the many aisles lining the store, searching for relics of the past. Things like—a handmade jam that tasted just like their grandma used to make, or a pie from one of the bakery shelves cooked with fresh ingredients that were now hard to find elsewhere and attention to detail. Marionberry pies were one of their biggest sellers.

These small comforts had drastically increased in value ever since the English world's pace had made the production of these goods virtually impossible. Only the

Amish were willing to spend seven hours churning a vat of honey butter. Good food required incredible patience, and from what Mary knew of the English world, things were dreadfully rushed in that way of life. Women were too busy holding down jobs to tend to their children, to teach them weaving and carpentry. Yet, for Mary's Amish sect, modernity was the enemy of virtue.

Like virtually everyone else in her community, Mary had enjoyed her Rumpspringa and had used every moment of her experimental life among the English to explore new things, and food was one of her top priorities.

Years ago, in a hospital, while visiting her dying grandfather she'd caught a few glimpses of a food magazine. Her entire life up until that point had consisted of her mother's simple yet delicious cooking. She knew nothing of food brought from faraway places like India and Asia, and she wanted to try them. Whatever money she'd been able to pocket during her break from the Amish, had gone towards small meals in restaurants and grocery stores. She'd been able to try fondue, and Paella, sushi and so much more. If she'd only had more time, perhaps she'd have been able to experience the nuances of French cuisine dancing across her palate. Yet, so many of the things she'd wanted to try had evaded her for lack of funds.

The experience was slightly marred, by the difficulties she and the other Amish teenagers had in surviving. Part of the Rumspringa ritual within her sect was that parents were meant to let go of their children so that they could explore the English world, first hand. With only twenty dollars in her pocket, Rumspringa also represented the worst possibilities of leaving the safety of her Amish community—like homelessness and a life of poverty.

Mary had banded together with a few friends and they'd all managed to obtain low paying jobs at a few nearby fast food joints, but the bills piled up higher and higher as all of them had fallen further and further behind. All of them were used to hard work, but at least within their small community, they'd work hard during the day and then come home to a safe place where they could eat and rest. Having menial jobs outside of the Amish community and having to pay for everything from food to high rent prices meant that staying afloat was almost impossible. Mary, as well as all of her friends had chosen to return back to their small Amish sect. Life in the English world was too hard.

Still, there were little things which had stayed with her from her time out in the English world. Mary had ripped one of the pages from a food and wine magazine and had stuffed it away in her apron. Each night, after finishing her chores, she often snuck away to the outhouse with a candle and sat in the darkness, just staring at the photograph, picking the various elements of the food apart. The English somehow even made a show of eating—and yet this was also a form of art. Not everything on an English plate was meant to be eaten, which was a novel concept to Mary. Some foods were garnish—which meant that they were intended only for show. The concept seemed wasteful to Mary, but also endlessly intriguing.

Mary pressed her hand to her belly again and reached down to grab a clothes pin. The wind rustled through the already- hanging sheets and she felt a strange wave of gratitude rush through her body. There was so much suffering in the world...but somehow, she had at least been born into a peaceful community. The Amish had problems, but at least they faced them together.

As Mary turned to go inside, at once, she saw him standing in the middle of her doorway wearing a black slack-vest.

Her heart thumped rapidly as she strained to take in the seriousness of the situation. It seemed totally impossible—like something out of a nightmare, that there would be a strange man in her house. Then, Mary saw it—a small handgun which was cocked and poised at the ready, aimed directly at her head.

The handgun was now aimed at the middle of her temple and his bloodshot eyes were filled with rage. Mary screamed and ducked, trying desperately to flee as the first blast cut through the air. Then, she ran right into her drying white sheets, tripping over her own feet as she covered the white linen in a huge amount of her blood.

She could hear the clop of his heavy boots as he descended from the porch, and walked over to where she lay in the yard. He seemed to be some kind of experienced killer and his lethality was evident in his bearing.

In the span of just a few seconds, a million thoughts raced through Mary's mind. Was he ex-Amish? Was a former customer from the store? She strained to try and place his face. There was something distantly familiar about him, but it was difficult to place him.

There was so much hardness and anger scrawled across his features that he looked more animal than human. Had the English world really become that hate-filled and dangerous? At that moment, Mary pitied him. She felt no anger towards him in her heart or soul. The man was obviously suffering, and what he needed was compassion and love.

She looked down at her stomach with a trembling hand. Blood was gushing out of the wound in her belly, and she felt panicked for the life of her unborn child. If God could only spare one of them; she hoped he'd somehow create a miracle to save her child, even though she was only a few weeks along.

The shooter was standing right over her now—the barrel of the gun, aimed at her temple. "Why?" Mary asked softly. "Do you even have a reason?" She asked again. She wasn't used to speaking to men so forcefully, but for some reason the words came out in a way she hadn't expected. The shooter paused for a moment, and then started to laugh at her snide remark.

Mary gripped at her stomach again. Maybe there was a chance to save the baby. "Don't do that!" The man screamed in a rage and Mary raised her hands out in front of her abdomen, defensively. "I'm sorry," she said. "It's just that if you kill me, these will be the last moments I ever share with my baby and I want him to feel loved." Her words made the man crack.

He lowered the gun and walked a few feet away from her and started to pace, talking to himself. Mary pressed one of the sheets to her stomach. She could feel contractions coming on now and was praying to God that she wouldn't miscarry.

"I keep screwing everything up!" The man shouted. Then he punched her white picket fence, accidentally driving a huge splinter into his knuckle. He screamed a few obscenities and started to kick the wall. Mary watched him for a moment, considering if he was far enough away that she might be about to flee. Then, she looked down. Even if her legs were able to carry her fast enough to escape his grasp, he might shoot her from behind. Plus, the twinge of contractions meant that she should try and remain as still as possible.

For some reason, the man's rage reminded Mary of her younger brother Noah. Whenever he'd burst into a fit of rage, her mother would cradle him close, kiss him on the forehead and sing him a song. Mary looked over at the distressed man, tears now streaming down his face. He ran a few muscled knuckles through his hair. Mary swallowed. "Do you want some pie?" Mary asked.

The idea seemed absurd. She didn't even know if she could walk, let alone hobble into the kitchen to retrieve a slice of pie, yet she decided to try. She groaned as she struggled to her feet, still bleeding, and went back into her house where she pulled out two white plates that clattered as she removed them gently from the cupboard. The shooter followed her inside and sat down while she placed a huge hunk of cherry pie in front of him with a weak grin.

Very slowly, the shooter picked up a fork and began to eat. Then, even more slowly, he began to talk.

He felt that the Amish had things too easy. He'd been laid off and had lost his health insurance. After his health coverage had been laid to ruin, his wife could no longer afford her dialysis treatments for kidney failure. She'd died while they were in the process of applying for state coverage. He'd written many letters of complaint to his senators, to the hospital that had denied treatment, and even to the governor, but they'd walled him off at every turn.

While drowning in that process, he'd lost all faith in mankind and had somehow gone rogue.

He'd managed to find out that the kidney transplant, which would have gone to his wife had instead been given to an elderly Amish person on medical assistance.

Mary slid a second piece of pie across the table. She watched as the man picked it up, breaking the crust off in his hand and putting it into his mouth.

"So, you blame the Amish for her death?' Mary asked. The shooter had put the gun down on the table flat as he considered his response. "I blame the system," the man said, looking up. "I blame the eighty-five-year-old who decided to take up a spot on the transplant list." Mary nodded silently. "You think that a person of advanced age should just be life to die?" Mary wanted to know. "When there aren't enough kidneys to go around, I do," he said softly, breaking off another chunk of pie, and swallowing. "It's an evil system," the man blurted out.

Mary cleared her throat. "Which system? The English system, or the Amish person that also needed help?" The man collapsed into a pile of sobs at the table, his hand shaking as it gripped the gun.

Just then, Mary heard the small bell which doubled as a door chime and she turned to see her husband Jacob step inside. She could clearly see the shock evident on his face as he took in the crazed man at the table and Mary's bleeding stomach. With a howl of anguish, Jacob ran towards the man at the table who now stood to meet the threat. Jacob lunged for his throat, but the man was quick with the handgun.

The sound of the blast rang out loudly and Mary fell to the floor, helpless to stop the horror around her. Before passing out from blood loss, Mary whispered a heartfelt prayer and hoped that God was listening.

Chapter 2

One year later.

Mary sat rocking the small bundle in her arms and listening to the soft cooing noises of her beautiful baby. After seven long months of bed rest and deep grief over the premature death of her beloved husband, Mary had finally given birth to a healthy baby girl. Several weeks early, the child had been small, but now little four-month-old Hope was just as happy and healthy as any other child in their Amish community.

Mary had feared losing both husband and child throughout her pregnancy despite the community's assurance to put her faith in God. She still trusted in his plan for her life, but at times she feared her own grief and fears would overwhelm her. Jacob had given his life to the gunman in order to save her and their baby. She only wished that he could have seen Hope grow up. Jacob would have made a wonderful father.

The gunman, in his remorse and grief had taken his own life that day in their kitchen, and Mary struggled daily with the amount of tragedy suffered on that horrible day. In addition to that, the Amish were beginning to whisper about the fact that she had not yet found a new husband to act as a father to Hope. To them, prolonged grief was sinful. Yet, Mary was beyond caring about the opinions of gossips. She needed to move slowly back into her life.

A soft knock on the door pulled Mary from her memories and she stood slowly, not wanting to wake the baby. The community had drawn together to help Mary throughout the past year and she opened the front door expecting one of the neighbors with a meal. Instead, she came face to face with a ghost from her past.

Mary drew in a startled breath as she stared at the man she had been promised to marry before Jacob. She could feel herself blush as she peered at his handsome chiseled features. Benjamin had been her first love and even now she could feel her heart flutter just at the sight of him. His deep set brown eyes and dark hair accented his strong jaw line, and even through his shirt she could see the outline of his abdominal muscles and biceps.

"Hello Benjamin, this is an unexpected surprise," Mary said softly. She invited him inside and felt her heart flutter when he agreed. Mary had heard that Benjamin was moving back into the community, but she hadn't realized it would happen so soon. She laid Hope into her bassinet and poured Benjamin a cup of Dutch tea from the kitchen.

She had so many questions to ask him, but was unsure of how to approach them. Benjamin had been one of the few teenagers not to return from his Rumspringa and the community had been devastated, including Mary. They were supposed to have been married the following fall. When Benjamin had not returned, Mary was left to deal with the loss in silence. The Amish did not talk about those who strayed from the faith. It was simply as though the person had never existed.

Instead of Benjamin, Mary had instead married Jacob and had quickly become pregnant. Now, for the second time in her life she was without a husband. Only this time, she had a baby to care for as well.

Benjamin took the glass of tea politely and took a seat when offered. Mary was just as pretty as he remembered and he was glad to be home. For three years, he had run from his people, his home, and his faith. When word finally got to him of Mary's predicament he knew it was time to stop running at last.

It had not been easy to earn his place back among the Amish, but now that he was here, he intended to fulfill his obligation and affection for Mary. "I hope you can forgive me the sins I committed against you when I was just an ignorant boy," Benjamin said. His voice was deeper now, and he spoke with such command that it made Mary blush. Mary paused for a moment. "There is nothing to forgive, Benjamin. You had every right to choose your own way."

Benjamin stayed for an hour reminiscing on times past and conversing lightly about the present. He found out that Mary had been unable to work during the later parts of her pregnancy (after the gun wound) and had been living solely off the support of the community. Now that she had given birth and both she and Hope were healthy, she would be required to return to her duties. With no father and husband, Mary's life would be difficult within the community to say the least.

Benjamin offered to come by the next day and help with the yard work and Mary gratefully accepted. A pain of guilt coursed through his body as he looked at Mary's smiling face. If not for his mistakes and choices, Mary would have been his wife, and Hope his child. Their suffering was in part because of him and he did not know how to ask forgiveness for such an offense.

With a slight nod of his head, Benjamin excused himself and promised to return in the morning. His eyes lingered for several more seconds on Mary's face, as he studied her features intently. Then, he turned to walk the mile back to his house.

After so many years away from his culture, the walk felt revitalizing in many ways. The feel of the fresh air against his face and the smell of grass brought back the joyous feelings he associated with his childhood. His life had not been easy since leaving the community and in many ways, he wished he had never left.

No matter what had happened in his time away, Benjamin always knew that this was where his heart lay. Here with his people, amongst family and friends and a way of life that brought peace. More than any of that though was the woman who still tugged upon his heart, calling him home. In the English world, he'd laid awake so many nights thinking about her, longing for her touch. None of the girls he'd met could compare to her kindness of virtue. For some reason, Mary was the standard by which Benjamin measured every other female.

Mary awoke the next morning, and after feeding and changing Hope she went to work baking fresh biscuits. By the time Benjamin arrived, the smell of breakfast was wafting along the morning breeze. She opened the door with a smile and offered Benjamin an invitation to eat with her. She was pleasantly grateful when he agreed.

As much as Mary had loved Jacob and been committed to him in every way, a part of her heart had always belonged to Benjamin and she couldn't help but notice those feelings blossom again when he was around. Their hands brushed for a moment as she handed him a platter of biscuits and her heart fluttered. Benjamin had let his fingertips linger on hers, at that made her core flood with a new sense of want. Benjamin smiled at her over the table and she felt safe for the first time in a long while.

After breakfast, Benjamin excused himself and went to work in the yard. The community had done much for Mary and Hope, but there were still many things that needed repairs and maintenance. Several of the fence posts needed to be reset and painted and their small vegetable field was in need of rotation.

Mary watched Benjamin work throughout the morning and carried him a fresh glass of tea to keep him cool while he labored in the sun. She set Hope down on a blanket smiling at the beautiful miracle in her midst. Hope was a joyful baby who rarely cried and Mary could clearly see a lot of Jacob in Hope's eyes, which was a reminder to her that he'd always be with her.

Occasionally Mary would glance up and see Benjamin staring back at her while he worked, and she wondered what his intentions might be, now that he had returned. There was a part of her that was very happy he had come back, but another part of her felt as though she were betraying Jacob in some way.

There were so many answers she still didn't have, but at the very least she was glad that Benjamin had found his way home. Benjamin jumped down from the she'd roof and made his way over to baby hope, where he easily scooped her into his strong arms. He tossed her up and down as she giggled. The scene made Mary's heart swell.

After Benjamin finished for the morning he said a quiet goodbye to Mary and Hope and headed out to do his own work for the day. He had agreed to work for his father's furniture business in the afternoons, making rocking chairs and cabinets. Building furniture had been one of the reasons Benjamin had left the Amish in the first place and he was glad to be back where his work was appreciated.

Benjamin had wanted to work in the English world making lots of money building and selling his own furniture, but none of his goals had worked the way he wanted them too.

Finding buyers who wanted handmade furniture in the English world was near to impossible. Benjamin would spend hours carving the intricate designs into his hand-crafted furniture piece by piece, only to find that a store down the street could produce a hundred pieces an hour for half the cost. The English frequented stores like Walmart and Ikea, where furniture was sold in droves.

No matter how many times Benjamin had explained that his quality of work was far superior to the manufactured furniture from the assembly lines, no one cared. He'd felt beaten down by the fact the that quality of his work didn't mean much in the English world.

Occasionally he would sell a single piece to an individual which would give him enough money to eat for a week or so, but there were many times when he went hungry as well. There were so many times when Benjamin had wanted to come home and resume his life in a place that appreciated his value, but his pride had stood in the way.

When he had learned of Mary's marriage to Jacob, he had seen no reason not to swallow his pride in order to return. Mary had always been the love of his life.

Now that Mary was alone, and raising a baby on her own, Benjamin knew the time had come for him to atone and make amends. In his heart, he had never stopped loving Mary and he could see that she still carried feelings for him too. He also knew that Mary had truly loved Jacob, and that the man had died defending her and their baby.

Benjamin was not looking to take Jacob's place in any way, he simply wanted to provide a good home and a proper future for Mary and Hope.

Throughout the next several months Benjamin and Mary resumed the friendship they had shared in their youth and Benjamin found the loneliness in his heart beginning to fade. When he held Hope in his arms, he felt alive in a way he had never before known, and when he peered into Mary's brown eyes he knew once again, the true meaning of peace.

One evening, he'd stayed on late at the farm and had goaded Mary into a dance with him. They were standing on the front porch, which was drenched in moonlight, and she'd never looked so beautiful. How could he not touch her? Ever so slowly, he'd placed his hands around her waist as they'd began to sway as Jacob sang her an old tune. When the song was over and they'd peeled their bodies apart, his heart was pounding a million times per minute. He felt so full of love that he feared he might burst. In the heat of the moment, he'd reached for her and had pressed his lips against hers.

Instead of pulling away, she had responded by draping her arms around his neck. "I love you Benjamin Johnson," he heard her whisper. He responded by kissing her on the cheek. "I've loved you since the first day I saw you," he said in his gruff voice. Then, from inside the small cottage Hope has started to cry. Benjamin watched in disbelief as Mary hurried away to tend to her child.

Chapter 3

Every morning Benjamin came and worked to help Mary establish herself once again and every afternoon he went to work making furniture for his father. He wanted nothing more than to make the arrangement permanent but he was afraid that Mary would not accept. After all, he'd broken her heart so many years ago. How could she ever learn to trust him again?

There were things about his life outside of the Amish community he had not shared with her as of yet, and he wondered if she would be able to accept him once she found out the truth. If he were to be a true husband to her and a good father to Hope, he would have to share that part of himself. It would not be fair of him to ask Mary to marry him under false pretenses. He would have to come clean.

Mary waited patiently in the living room bouncing Hope softly on her lap. Benjamin had asked to see her again this evening after his work was done and she had accepted. Over the last several months since Benjamin's return, she had allowed herself to cautiously renew the friendship with him they had once shared.

At times, she could tell that he was willing to offer her more, but he seemed hesitant to ask. She herself was not sure that she was ready for the commitment once again. The loss of Benjamin once and then the loss of Jacob had damaged her in so many ways. She was not sure she was willing or even able to open her heart for another. If she were though, the thought of it being with Benjamin felt like the right choice.

Every time Mary watched Benjamin with Hope, she felt her heart soar as though maybe God was giving her back some of what she had lost. When Jacob had been killed a part of Mary had died as well and she felt as though she would never be able to love another. With Benjamin, she felt as though she were at least ready to try again.

Mary heard the knock on the door and stood letting Benjamin inside. She had prepared herself as best as possible for what she thought he was going to ask her—to marry.

Slowly, Benjamin entered the sitting room with a pale face. In his hand, he held his hat, and today he seemed unable to make eye contact as he sat across from her on the sofa, clearing his through. "I'm sure you know by now, Mary, that I have serious feeling for you." He seemed to tremble as he spoke. "Before I can ask if you'll accept my hand, I need to tell you something very important. I hope you'll be able to love me in spite of it."

Mary leaned back in her chair, listening intently. Tears seemed to swell up in Benjamin's eyes. "One of the ways I made a living in the English world as an orderly at the hospital." He swallowed, seeming to choke on his own statements. "When I learned that Jed's wife Rebekah was in need of a kidney, I made changes to the organ transplant list. That shooter's wife was still on the list—the insurance hadn't actually removed her. I did that. I killed her."

The words felt like daggers piercing her heart. "You took that man's wife off the kidney transplant list?" Mary repeated. Benjamin nodded. "I had access to many of the files. I switched some of the paperwork so that it would look like his wife had been dropped by her insurance company, when she actually had another 30 days left on it. I didn't know how serious it was. I didn't know that she's die as a result."

Rage pulsated through Mary's body. Beautiful sweet Benjamin hadn't been simply acting out of the kindness of his heart, but to ease a guilty conscience. He was the reason that the shooter's wife had died, and he was also the reason that her husband Jacob had been targeted. Mary let out a wail that could have woken the dead, and Benjamin rushed to his feet to catch her.

"Don't touch me!" She screamed. "Get your filthy hands off me!" Mary shouted. Yet, even with the knowledge that he'd committed a grave sin, his hands felt like butter on her skin. She could see the remorse in his eyes—and yet his horrible stupid decision has resulted in so much death.

Benjamin dropped to his knees. "Please Mary...please forgive me." He said through a veil of tears. He sobbed loudly and was drenching her shirt. Mary looked up and smacked him hard across the face. Benjamin flew back, stunned. "Go tell them what you've done. Go tell everyone what you've done, or I will!" Mary shrieked. Benjamin continued to hold tightly to her skirt while sobbing.

Then, suddenly he stood and turned to go. "You made me love you again," Mary blurted out. He turned to face her. "I never stopped loving you and I never will. "

Chapter 3

Benjamin did as he was told and reported his crime to the bishop who hen reported him to the English authorities. After two lengthy trials, he was found guilty of forgery and placed on probation—a status which destroyed his honor within the community, but he seemed to learn the many lessons that followed.

Despite it all, Benjamin wordless crept onto Mary's farm each morning and did the work—milking the cows and working the fields, before returning to his own. After the first month, he left her a small hand-made card, again begging for forgiveness.

He'd gone to the shooter's family too and had explained his part in what happened. Of course, he hadn't been responsible for the murderer's decision to pick up a gun and start killing people, but he had caused that man incredible pain by inadvertently causing the death of his wife. Slowly, months turned to years, and Mary was eventually able to see the Benjamin was sincere. He would spend the rest of his life trying to make amends if he had to.

About six months later, she'd invited him into the house for dinner again. "You can never lie to me or anyone else ever again," Mary had said, sipping on a glass of cool lemonade. "You can never be that person you became in the English world again, because that person was a monster." Mary said. She could already see tears streaming down Benjamin's face.

"Will it ever be possible for me to earn your love back? Will you ever be able to love me again?" Benjamin asked. "I never stopped loving you," Mary answered quietly "Not after you skipped out on our wedding, not after all the horrible things you've done. I have loved you through ever second of it."

Mary got up from the table, walked around it and sat down on his lap. Ever so slowly, she kissed the tears already wet on his face. "I thought that maybe if I came home, I could make things right," Benjamin muttered. "But when I came home you were the only thing I could see. You've always been my home, Mary. You're my very soul." "Then do right by me and do right by yourself. Forgiveness is not found in the words you speak, but the things you do."

Mary had been flabbergasted when Benjamin took it upon himself to help sick people. He registered as a donor and gave up one of his kidneys, as well as a significant amount of bone marrow. He was using his very body to make amends, and while he could never go back and undo his crime, he'd made sure that three different families were spared the grief of losing loved ones. The months rolled by and Mary could see the changes in him—that his mistakes had somehow deepened him and made him more human.

It was late in the evening when he'd come to her home, knocking on the door. She answered in her nightgown and he'd pulled her own into the cold night air, laughing. Then, he dropped to one knee. "Mary me," Benjamin blurted out. Mary approached him slowly. She undid the buttons on his shirt until they fell away, revealing the huge scar across his abdomen...one he'd earned from donating a kidney. Then, she unbuckled his belt and felt the scar on his thigh—earned from donating bone marrow twice. Then, Mary looked into his eyes. He'd been a foolish young man, but he was now someone new. Someone she could trust. But he was always someone she'd loved with all her heart. She loved him then, and she'd love him forever.

CALL OF THE AMISH

ELIZA FITZGERALD

Part One:

The call came in the middle of the night. Somehow Elizabeth King's daed had heard the telephone ringing in his shop, and had hurried from bed to answer it. He had the only phone for miles around, and often when the phone rang there was an emergency that needed tending to, though just as often someone from the community hurried to their house to use the phone as well.

"Elizabeth, wake up, my girl."

Elizabeth squinted into the sudden brightness, and for a moment she was so disoriented that she had no idea where she was or who was talking to her. Then she realized that her maemm was kneeling beside her bed with a kerosene lantern shining.

"What is it, Maemm?" Elizabeth asked.

"Your cousin, Melissa, she needs your help," her maemm replied. "Her babe is coming early, and there isn't enough time to get her to the birthing center that she chose in the city. She's refusing to go to the local hospital, and you're the only midwife she knows. Hurry now, and get dressed, girl. Your daed is getting the buggy ready to take you."

Elizabeth felt her eyes go wide and round as she drew in a sharp breath. Thoughts whirred through her mind as she slipped from beneath the covers of her bed, careful not to jostle her sister, Sarah, who grumbled in her sleep and turned toward the wall. As Elizabeth slipped into her dress and tucked her hair up into her kapp, she looked at her maemm.

"I don't know if I'm ready for this, Maemm," she whispered, feeling her stomach form into a tight knot.

"The Lord has delivered you to this point," her maemm said. "Pray that He will guide your work, and remember that all you do is in the glory of His name."

Elizabeth nodded, kissed her maemm on the cheek, and hurried down the stairs to get her shawl from where it hung on a peg by the front door. Her daed was already in the driver seat of the buggy, waiting in the moonlight to drive her quickly into town where her Englischer cousin was waiting for her.

As her daed drove along shadowy lanes, Elizabeth bowed her head, and silently prayed, *"Dear Lord, I am scared. I have never done this by myself before, and I need You to be with me. I need You to guide my hands. Please lift up Melissa and her unborn babe. Let me be an instrument of Your peace. Let me do this well, Lord. Please, oh, please. Amen."*

When she got done with her prayer, she clenched her fists together on her lap, pulling her shawl tighter around her shoulders. Elizabeth had never been so terrified of anything in her whole life, but at the same time she felt a sense of peace descend upon her. In that moment, she knew, she just knew that the Lord had heard her prayer. He had created her for this moment.

Her daed pulled the buggy up in front of Melissa's house, the electric laws all blazing, and Melissa's husband, Jim, on the front porch, pacing. When he caught sight of her, he jogged down the stairs, and put his arm around her. "Elizabeth! I'm so glad that you are here," Jim said. "She's saying that she's going to have the baby any moment."

"Did you get the items together that were on the birthing center's list?" Elizabeth asked, calmly.

Jim nodded, his head bobbing up and down. He looked so helpless that Elizabeth felt sorry for him. She shrugged out of her shawl and handed it to him. "Good," Elizabeth said, rolling up her sleeves. "Are you going to stay in the room? I'm sure that Melissa would find that helpful."

"Anything," Jim said. "Just tell me what I need to do, and I'll do it."

Taking a deep breath, Elizabeth walked into the bedroom where Melissa was moaning softly as she lay on the bed. With a quick glance at her cousin, all of Elizabeth's cool, collected calm seemed to flee. She murmured another quick prayer.

"Hello, cousin," Elizabeth said in a soft tone as she entered the darkened room. She paused to allow her cousin to register her appearance, but also to gauge the situation that lay before her. "Melissa," she continued in a firmer voice. "You are going to be just fine. I'm going to open these curtains to let in some light." Elizabeth wasn't sure why, but it felt right to let light in. Her mind flickered to one of her favorite Bible verses [something about letting your light shine]

When Elizabeth got closer to the bed, Melissa opened her eyes and reached out to grip Elizabeth's hand. "Thank you for coming," Melissa said through gritted teeth as another contraction ripped through her small body. "Lizzy, I don't know if I can do this."

Hearing her cousin call her by her childhood nickname brought Elizabeth soundly into the present, and a sense of peace descended on her. She reached out and smoothed her cousin's sweaty curls away from her forehead. "You can do this," she said. "And you will."

Part Two:

"It was the most amazing experience I've ever had, Paul," Elizabeth said with a contented sigh as she leaned back against the seat of Paul's buggy. She could still feel the rush of adrenaline that had coursed through her veins as Melissa pushed the baby girl out into Elizabeth's hands. When she had handed the baby to her cousin, tears had run rivulets down both of their cheeks. Jim had cut the cord, and beamed with the pride of a new father, though Elizabeth had caught the relief in his eyes too. He hadn't been able to stop thanking her.

"I just know that this is what God brought me into the world to do," she added. Then she turned to her beau, the boy she had grown up with, fallen in love with, and expected to marry as soon as he took over his daed's farm. She expected to see her own excitement reflected in his eyes; he had always been her biggest cheerleader, especially as she had embarked on her journey to become a midwife.

Instead, Paul gazed at her with serious eyes and his mouth drawn into a tight frown. "Elizabeth," he said, drawing out the syllables of her name as he often did when he thought she was being silly.

"What?" she asked, her eyebrows furrowing. She thought that Paul would have been excited for her. She thought he would have seen the importance of the event through her eyes. She had thought they had the same vision for their future. It seemed to her now that she thought wrong.

"God brought you into the world to be my wife," Paul said softly.

Elizabeth's confusion amplified. There was a buzzing in her ears that she didn't like. "God created me to be many things," she said, her breath feeling hollow in her chest.

"Of course," Paul said in a cajoling tone, but something in his expression made her think that he didn't believe that.

"You know that I can't wait to be your wife," Elizabeth said. "But the feeling I got delivering Melissa's baby, well, I can't even describe it. There are no words for being a witness to a miracle like that. Doing that over and over would be an amazing way to live."

Paul turned toward her in the carriage seat. He reached out to take her hands in his own. "Elizabeth, it's fine for you to do midwife work right now, but what happens after we get married? You'll have a household to run. And what happens when we begin to have children?"

The starkness of his words made Elizabeth pause. She knew that he had a point, and she wasn't going to disagree with him on that point. But she wasn't willing to concede that she should give up being a midwife just because her life would be busier.

Slowly she said, "I can't wait to have a home and children of our own, but I just can't see how being a midwife wouldn't be able to fit into that picture."

Paul pressed his lips together. "You'll simply be too busy." He said it in a tone that made it clear that he thought that was all there was to say on the matter, but that fact made Elizabeth even more upset.

"God doesn't just create us for one purpose," Elizabeth said. "I'm sorry, Paul, but I just don't think that I agree with you."

The look on Paul's face went from disapproving to impassive. Elizabeth had never seen him act like this before, and she didn't like it one bit. "I think you should take me home now," she said, drawing her hand away. Turning her face away from him, she pressed her lips together. If she said something now, she knew that there was a chance that she would say something that she would regret.

Paul didn't move for a long moment. So long, in fact that Elizabeth almost looked over at him, but instead she held firm. Finally he heaved a sigh, and flicked the reins. As the buggy moved off down the road, Elizabeth felt a rush of tears flood her eyes. Blinking rapidly so they wouldn't fall, she tried to figure out a way to make Paul understand where she was coming from, but her mind was a blank.

Instead she decided to pray. *"Dear Lord, I don't understand what is happening right now. Paul has always been my soul mate, the one that I know I'm destined to be with. And yet, today I know that You showed me another part of Your plan for me. How do I make Paul see this? How do I explain it? The feeling that delivering Melissa's baby gave me? Where are you leading me, Lord? Please show me the way. Amen."*

When she finished praying, Elizabeth felt a sense of peace descend on her. She drew a deep breath, and said, "Paul, I don't know how to explain this feeling to you, but I know that what I did today came from God. I don't want things to be bad between us, but right now this is the path that He is leading me down. I...I think that we should spend a bit of time apart."

"How can you say that?" Paul asked with a gruffness in his voice that Elizabeth knew well. He did that when he was trying to keep the hurt at bay. She had never caused him pain before, and the realization made her heart ache. Yet she wasn't going to back off.

"I just know in my heart that if we're going to have a future together then we need to trust in the Lord and His plan for us," Elizabeth said.

Just as she finished speaking, the buggy turned into the drive for Elizabeth's house. When Paul reined the horse in, Elizabeth was quick to get out on her own. She hurried into the house without looking back. She needed to keep her resolve, and she knew that if she looked back, her heart might break.

Part Three:

"Gross-mammi? Can I talk to you?" Elizabeth leaned on the kitchen door jamb of her grandmother's house.

"Of course, dear," her gross-mammi said, glancing over her shoulder at her. She continued to mix the butter into the flour for the pie crust that she was making.

Elizabeth grabbed an apron off a hook on the wall as she entered the kitchen, and tied it around her waist. One of the rules about entering Gross-mammi's kitchen was that one had to help when they came in. No matter what. No matter who. Elizabeth had never minded. She found the act of baking with her grandmother soothing.

Reaching for a paring knife, Elizabeth began to slice strawberries for the berry pie her grandmother was preparing. "I delivered my cousin Melissa's baby yesterday," she said.

"Your daed told me," Gross-mammi said with a nod. "I'm proud of you, my girl. That's God's work."

Elizabeth felt a burst of joy in her chest. "I felt like God was touching my hands," she said, tears welling at the memory. "I can't think of a better way to describe it."

She finished cutting the strawberries, added them to the bowl with the blueberries and raspberries, and poured in a cup of sugar. As she was coating the berries her grandmother reached across the counter, and tapped her hand. Elizabeth glanced up at her beloved gross-mammi, and she could see the question in the older woman's eyes.

With a sigh, Elizabeth wiped her hands on her apron, and said, "I'm having a problem with Paul." As soon as she said the words, tears flooded her eyes. Unable to keep them in, they ran rivulets down her cheeks. Swiping at them with the heels of her hands, Elizabeth slumped over the counter, leaning her elbows on the floury surface.

"Oh, is that all?" Gross-mammi asked, waving her hand in the air. Elizabeth looked at her grandmother with surprise. The older woman continued, "A little lovers' spat, no?"

Elizabeth swiped at her leaky eyes again. "I don't know," she said unable to keep the misery out of her voice. "He doesn't like the idea of my being a midwife. At least not after we get married. If we get married, I guess. I just couldn't get him to understand how much I feel like God has called me to deliver babies, to be His hands in the world. Am I wrong, Gross-mammi?"

Her grandmother was silent, silent and still for a long time before she picked up the bowl of berries and poured them into the pie crust. Finally she said, "I think that only the Lord can answer that question, my dear. My advice to you is to pray. Pray hard, and then listen. Listen with all your heart and soul. If you do that, then I'm sure that you will find the answer that you seek."

Watching her grandmother put the pie into the oven, Elizabeth felt peace descend upon her. She knew that her gross-mammi's advice was sound and true. She did need to pray. And yet...right now she also needed her grandmother's comforting presence. And she needed pie.

"Is there any cleaning you need done, Gross-mammi?" Elizabeth asked. If she could distract herself by helping her grandmother, then she could perhaps calm her racing mind down enough to let her soul catch up. Then she could pray.

"Would you mind bringing down the rugs, and giving them a good beating?" Elizabeth was sure that she could see a smile hovering around her gross-mammi's mouth. The rugs probably didn't need to be beaten, but Elizabeth was glad for the opportunity to work out some of her frustration.

"Of course," Elizabeth said as she headed into the front room to get the first rug. Rolling it up, she hefted it over her shoulder.

Over and over, Elizabeth retrieved rug after rug, hung them on the clothesline, and beat the dust and dirt out of them. By the time she was done, she was exhausted and sweaty, but she also felt calmer. After she had placed the last rug back in the upstairs guest bedroom, Elizabeth jogged back down the stairs.

"All done, Gross-mammi," she called as she came into the kitchen.

"Just in time," her grandmother said. "The pie just came out of the oven. Come, sit with me, and we'll have a slice."

"Great," Elizabeth said with a grin.

The two women sat together, and for a long stretch of time Elizabeth felt soothed, which was exactly what she had hoped to feel when she came here. But then thoughts of Paul started to creep back in. By the time she was taking her last bite of pie, she was having trouble swallowing. As if her gross-mammi could read her thoughts, she reached over and patted Elizabeth's hand again.

"Just remember to pray," Gross-mammi said. "The Lord will give you all the answers that you need. Just a moment." Elizabeth threaded her hands together as she watched her grandmother leave the room. A moment later she returned with a large Bible in her hands.

Opening it, she said, "I think this will help you. Ecclesiastes 3: 1-8, 'To every thing there is a season, and a time to every purpose under the heaven 2 A time to be born, and a time to die; a time to plant, and a time to pluck up that which is planted;3 A time to kill, and a time to heal; a time to break down, and a time to build up;4 A time to weep, and a time to laugh; a time to mourn, and a time to dance;5 A time to cast away stones, and a time to gather stones together; a time to embrace, and a time to refrain from embracing;6 A time to get, and a time to lose; a time to keep, and a time to cast away;7 A time to rend, and a time to sew; a time to keep silence, and a time to speak;8 A time to love, and a time to hate; a time of war, and a time of peace.'"

"I've always liked that one," Elizabeth agreed. As she kissed her grandmother goodbye, Elizabeth felt calm once again. She needed to pray.

Part Four:

Dear Lord, Elizabeth prayed as she walked toward her closest friend, Miriam's, house. *I know that You are the designer of my life. I want to trust in the path that You have laid out for me. I believe, Lord, help me in my unbelief. I know that I am a sinner, and that I try to assert my own will instead of listening to You. I want to change, though, Lord. I ask you to show me what path You want for me. Should I be a midwife? Or should*

I marry Paul? Or...Lord, I know that it is asking a lot, but is there a way that I could have both? I'm listening, Lord. Show me the way. Amen.

Elizabeth swallowed as she finished her prayer. It wasn't that prayer was foreign to her; she prayed often and with fervent sincerity. She had meant what she had prayed, that she was a sinner who all too often tried to fit her will onto that of the Lord's. But she had also meant her plea for help. Now she had to clear her head—and heart—to listen and hear the Lord's answer.

By the time she got to Miriam's house, Elizabeth still felt as confused as ever. She couldn't help feeling like she wanted to press the Lord for an answer right now, but she knew all that would get her was a lesson in being patient.

"Elizabeth!"

Miriam clattered down the front steps, and threw her arms around Elizabeth. For a moment all of her stress melted away as she hugged her friend back. This was what she needed, desperately. Perhaps that was why she had felt such an overwhelming desire to visit Miriam today. The thought occurred to her so fast that Elizabeth almost missed it. Maybe this was the Lord answering some part of her prayer. Maybe she needed to listen to what Miriam had to say. Miriam had gone through more in her young life than most people would in all their years so Elizabeth definitely trusted her friend's perspective.

"My maemm told me that you delivered your cousin's baby," Miriam said. "How wonderful! Come sit in the garden, and I'll go get some lemonade and cookies. You'll have to tell me all about it."

Elizabeth smiled, feeling relief wash over her. "Let me help," she said.

With a firm shake of her head, Miriam said, "Go sit in the garden. You're my guest. Let me get the refreshments."

Knowing that it was futile to argue with Miriam, Elizabeth headed toward the garden as her friend went to the house. Miriam and her family lived on the edge of their small town on a large farmette. Miriam's daed owned a popular furniture shop that was busy with tourists all through the summer months.

Chickens scattered as Elizabeth crossed the stone path toward the large kitchen garden that Miriam's maemm had spent years cultivating. Elizabeth sat down at the small wicker table set under a big willow tree. A moment later Miriam joined her.

Setting the lemonade and cookies under the tree, Miriam said, "So, tell me all about it. How was it delivering a baby for the first time?"

"It was beyond anything I can even explain," Elizabeth said, feeling a rush of pleasure as she remembered the experience. "It was like...like I was actually the Hands of God. Like He was guiding all my movements. I loved every second of it. I can't wait to do it again." Her smile faded as she thought about Paul.

"What's wrong?" Miriam asked, clearly seeing her friend's sudden distress.

Elizabeth sighed. "Paul wasn't very happy with my first experience."

"Why not?" Miriam held out the plate of cookies toward Elizabeth.

"He doesn't think that I can do both midwifery and being his wife," she said.

"Did he propose?" Miriam asked around a mouthful of cookie, her eyes widening.

Shaking her head, Elizabeth said, "No. I'm sure he's going to one day. Probably sooner rather than later, but he might not since he doesn't like the idea of my being a midwife. I wish that I could make him understand that what I'm doing when I deliver babies is God's work. I don't feel like it would detract from my duties as his wife."

Miriam bit into another cookie, and tipped her head to one side as she appeared to consider the situation. Elizabeth sucked in her breath as she waited to hear what her friend thought. What if Miriam felt the same way as Paul? That would only add to her confusion. The suspense grew as the silence stretched, and Elizabeth felt a knot tighten in her stomach.

Finally Miriam said, "I'm sure that Paul feels scared."

Her words shocked Elizabeth for a moment. Then she furrowed her brow, and said, "What do you mean?"

Taking a sip of her lemonade, Miriam shrugged. "It seems pretty clear to me. God has given you an incredible gift. You've found your calling. Most people wait their entire lives to find their calling. Paul has thought of you as his calling for your whole lives. To be married to you is what he is called to do."

"I always thought that too," Elizabeth said softly. "And I still do. I just wonder...can't God call us to more than one thing."

"Of course," Miriam said, waving her hand in the air. "There is a season for everything, so why can't we have more than one calling in our lives."

"My gross-mammi said almost the exact same thing," Elizabeth said. "I just wish that I could make Paul understand that."

"Maybe it's not so much about making Paul understand, but putting the situation entirely in God's hands," Miriam said.

"What do you mean?" Elizabeth wiped the cookie crumbs off her skirt as she looked at her friend.

"Well, you just need to do your best at what God is asking of you right now," Miriam said. "Paul needs to do the same. When the Lord is ready for the two of you to be together, you will be."

"You're so smart," Elizabeth told her friend. "I knew there was a reason that I wanted, no, needed, to come here today."

Miriam grinned at her. "You know I'm always here to help you if you need it," she said.

Elizabeth squeezed her friend's hand. She did know, and more than that she knew that the Lord had given her such a friend just for situations like this. She whispered a quick prayer of thanks before she reached for another cookie.

Part Five:

"I don't understand why you won't come out with me today," Paul said.

Looking at him as he stood at the bottom of the porch steps made Elizabeth's heart ache, but she had to keep in mind the advice that Gross-mammi and Miriam had given her. She had to follow God's plan for her, and she needed to stay strong on that. If that didn't mean that Paul was a part of that right now, then she needed to accept that and be strong.

"Because there's a baby over at the Hoestetler homestead that needs to be delivered," Elizabeth explained.

Paul frowned up at her. "I thought you had decided not to do midwifery anymore."

"Jean is one of my very best friends. You know that. Of course I need to be there." Elizabeth returned Paul's frown. The ache in her heart increased and stole her breath. Why would God let her feel so much pain? Cause so much pain between the two of them? Elizabeth knew that He was a good and loving God, so why would it be that He would allow such heartache to exist in the world?

And yet, Elizabeth knew that pain existed because of the sin of Adam and Eve. She was a sinner, so why should she expect any special treatment? "Paul," she said in a soft voice, "I truly believe that this is what God is calling me to do right now. I can't say if this is what God will always ask me to do, and I do think that you and I are called to be together, but I need to answer His call."

Paul's frown deepened, but he didn't argue with her. Instead he seemed to be listening to what she had to say. Finally he asked, "So what does that mean for us right now?"

"Right now?" Elizabeth repeated. She could sense the hurt in Paul, and she thought of what Miriam had said. If he was hurting as much as she was, then she didn't want to make it worse. "I think it means that we both need to pray deeply, and listen with all our hearts to what the Lord is telling us. Then we follow His plan, His path, His will for our lives. When it's time for us to come back together, He will let us know."

Paul nodded. "Can I still come to see you every Sunday?" he asked in a cracking voice that shattered Elizabeth's voice.

"Of course," she said. "And we'll keep talking about where God is leading us."

Elizabeth tried hard to put the whole conversation with Paul out of her mind as she delivered Sarai's baby that afternoon. Her good friend Jean helped, but seemed nervous to be attending her own sister's labor. After the little boy had been placed safely in his mother's arms, Elizabeth sank into a sofa in the parlor. Jean brought her a glass of tea and a muffin.

Jean sat down on a chair nearby, and the two of them ate in contented silence. When they were done, Elizabeth said, "I definitely know that God is leading me down this path right now."

The curious look on Jean's face made Elizabeth giggle, though she suspected that she was really just very tired. Elizabeth explained, "I've been praying that God would show me my path in life. I feel called to two such paths actually. Being a midwife is what I'm supposed to do right now, but I know that one day I'll marry Paul. I think that he is finally starting to understand that we can't impose our will on God's plans for us."

"That's not something we can ever do, is it?" Jean said.

"The thing that really bothers me about the whole situation," Elizabeth said, "is that Paul is so hurt by it all, and that's truly not what I want."

"You aren't hurting him on purpose," Jean said as if this was a fact that was obvious. "Unfortunately God's plan, if you truly want to submit to His will, bypasses all other plans."

"I know," Elizabeth agreed. "But do you suppose that there is a way to lessen his pain?"

Jean considered the question. "I'm sure that you are already doing it, but I would advise you to pray. Pray hard and listen hard."

Elizabeth nodded seriously. "I have been, and I'll continue to do it."

"Do you think that God is asking you to take some part away from each other for a while?" Jean asked.

The adrenaline from the delivery was wearing off, leaving Elizabeth with a bone deep exhaustion setting in. "No, I don't think that at all," she said.

"So, can't you just keep spending time together? And when it's time for the two of you to get married, you'll just know," Jean suggested.

"I guess I hadn't really thought about that," Elizabeth said with a frown. "That seems quite stupid of me, doesn't it?"

Jean shrugged. "Sometimes the most obvious solutions evade us."

"My biggest problem is that I don't know if Paul will feel the same way," Elizabeth said. "He's been so hurt by my midwifery."

"Maybe he just needs time to get used to it," Jean said. "You've just started. How many babies have you delivered so far?"

"Just two," Elizabeth said.

"Then time will help him accept this part of your life," Jean said firmly.

Elizabeth felt better as soon as Jean spoke. "You know, Jeannie, you are so smart."

Jean grinned at her. "I know," she replied. "But thanks that's nice of you to say."

As Elizabeth sank back into the sofa and felt her eyes drift closed, she offered up a prayer of thanks to the Lord that He had given her such good friends and advisors. How did she deserve such good things?

Part Six:

Three more babies were delivered in the next three weeks, and Elizabeth felt more certain than ever that God had called her to be a midwife. Things between her and Paul had been different, but not as bad as she had feared. Though he had been visiting less often, the visits that they did have seemed better to her. If pressed, she wasn't sure she would have been able to say exactly what seemed better, though there were little signs that Paul was beginning to understand how much being a midwife meant to her.

So when Paul pulled up the driveway in a new buggy, Elizabeth felt her heart stir with excitement and delight. She came out onto the porch as he jumped down. "What do you think?" he asked with an easy grin that she hadn't seen in weeks.

"It's lovely," she said. "When did you get it?"

"Yesterday," Paul said. He was happy, his eyes crinkling in the corners. There was a giddy energy coming off of him that reminded her of a child. "Can you come for a ride? Right now?"

Elizabeth laughed. She couldn't help it. He looked so happy. "Let me just grab my shawl."

Paul helped her up into the buggy. "Isn't it roomy?" he asked when they were both settled.

Glancing at the back seat, Elizabeth nodded. "It's great. It must have cost you a fortune," she said.

"I've been saving for it for a while," Paul admitted. "Actually I was praying that God would show me the right time to buy it, and recently I felt that it was time."

"I'm glad," Elizabeth said. She felt a momentary flash of surprise and disappointment that she wasn't included in the decision making process. Then she realized that Paul was doing exactly what she had asked him to do. He was listening for God's will in his life just as she had been doing in hers. The part of her that had felt so jealous of his decision a moment before suddenly rejoiced in it.

"It's big for a good reason," Paul was saying. Elizabeth realized with a guilty start that she hadn't been paying attention as he waxed lyrical about the many wonderful features of the buggy, which she was sure was top of the line. Paul probably had a reason for every choice that he had made; that was one of the many qualities that she loved about him.

"Oh?" Elizabeth said.

He nodded, and gave her a smile even as they lapsed into silence. They drove to the top of the highest hill in the county. The two of them had been coming here since they had first started courting, and Elizabeth still felt it was the most romantic place she could ever imagine.

As Paul pulled the horse to a stop, he half turned on the bench seat so that he was mostly facing her. "My maemm told me that you delivered another baby yesterday," he said. "How is that going?"

Elizabeth couldn't keep the surprise from her face as she said, "Amazing. It's still amazing."

Paul was quiet for such a long time that Elizabeth thought that he might be trying to come up with yet another way to talk her out of continuing to pursue being a midwife. Then he ran a hand along the back of his neck. "I'm sorry," he said. "I was wrong to try to stop you from doing something that you are so obviously meant to do. The truth is, well, the truth is that I was scared. I was scared that if you found something that was more important than me that I might lose you forever."

Miriam and Jean had been spot on with their assessment of the situation. Elizabeth reached across the seat to take Paul's hand. "I'm sorry that I didn't stop to listen to you and your concerns," she said. "I mean, really listen. The way you deserved."

"That's partly my fault. I was so blinded by my fears that I pressed you for something that I had no right to ask. I should have been listening to the Lord first, and then talking to you about everything in a calm and open manner," Paul said.

"Thank you for that," Elizabeth said. "But I think that what I should have said is that I understand that change can be scary, but also that I don't think God gives us just one calling in our lives. I think that He calls us to different things throughout our lives."

"That's a faithful thought," Paul said.

"Miriam planted that seed for me. I've been praying about it for weeks, and I see that the more I pray and listen, the more paths I can see that God is leading me down," Elizabeth said.

"God does call us down many paths," Paul agreed. "I see that now."

"I'm glad," Elizabeth said.

"And that's why I bought this buggy," Paul said.

Elizabeth's eyebrows knit together in confusion. "What do you mean?"

"This buggy is big enough for a family," Paul said. "I've been praying about it for a while now, and I felt led to buy it now."

"Paul, what are you saying?" Elizabeth asked as her breath caught in her chest.

"I'm asking if you will marry me," Paul said. Before she could answer, he rushed on, "I know what I said before, but I see now that you being a midwife is what God wants for you right now, and that doesn't take anything away from our marriage, if you'll say yes that is."

Blood pulsed through Elizabeth's veins triple time, and there was a rushing sound in her ears. She had been praying so hard for this very thing, and now that it was happening she knew that she needed to pray. *Lord, please show me what You have planned for me. Amen.*

As Paul reached over to take her other hand, he said, "And I know now that you should deliver babies as long as you can, as long as the Lord wills it. I will never stand in your way again."

That was the answer to her prayer. She opened her eyes wide as tears pooled in the corners, and she whispered, "Yes. I will marry you, Paul."

Paul leaned over to seal their engagement with a kiss, and Elizabeth felt God's peace descend upon her. She was glad that the two of them had gone through this rough patch because now she knew how to listen for God's will in her life. And that was the most valuable thing she could ever hope to learn.

www.ingramcontent.com/pod-product-compliance
Lightning Source LLC
Chambersburg PA
CBHW031419150726
47989CB00002B/722